THE CONSPIRACY FOR PEACE

(A 60'S FANTASY)

DAVID CRESSWELL

The Conspiracy for Peace

tellwell

Tellwell Talent
www.tellwell.ca

ISBN
978-0-2288-3999-6 (Hardcover)
978-0-2288-3998-9 (Paperback)

Table of Contents

PART 6:

The Field of Opportunity 199

Dedication

At the insistence of my wife and partner, Gail, this book was written. Thank you for your love and for believing in me. I could not have done it without you.

To my four children, you gave my life purpose and fulfilment.

Acknowledgements: Hello, I Love You

When I began to think that this story might become reality, I started to realize how many people have impacted my life. As this may be my one and only chance to 'write a long letter to all the friends I've known', bear with me.

To Chuck Davis, David Streib, Paul Rice, Mary Pattinson and my sister Deb: true friends are a treasure and I was blessed with a few. The bond is forever and unconditional.

My love of Shakespeare and the written word was inspired by my high school teacher, Mr. Roddy. He took me to the Black Swan coffee house. He showed me another world.

I knew a few wise men who believed in me, encouraged my dreams and changed my thinking. Paul Brackenbury gave me my first Bob Dylan album. Victor Ujimoto, my sociology professor, aspired to a better world and urged us to do the same. Professor Phidd told the truth. Dr. Henry Wiseman treated me like a son and showed me that true political protest is based on deeply felt values.

With authority must come wisdom, empathy and understanding. Mr. Cunniff, my high school principal, has those qualities in spades. I used his example many times in my career. Don Rikley, my superintendent, and friend gave me his support and encouragement when I needed it most.

To my fellow college conspirators, Doug Millington, John Millington, Rod Hewer, Olga Netchay, and my brother and sister for a time, Caesar and Margi, I owe my eternal thanks for your friendship.

My best friend and his girl, Peter Tabakoff and Susan Leitch, loved me and everything I am, and very much showed me how to love life.

Rob Douglas found me when I needed a friend. And he was a very good friend. He had a sparkle in his eye that kept life around him always interesting.

I had a family of friends who sustained me. They loved me for all my wild ideas which none of them held and gave me a home. To Winston and Sandra Mick, Jay and Linda McLaren, John and Gwen Rutland, Ken and Pat Houles, Bill and Cheryl Jackson and the rest of our group, those Dylan parties were real and I love you for that.

One of my newest friends and one of the best is Steve Reaume. He shared with me his guitar skills and so much more. He and Cindy could live in Earthborn. You are in the book.

Coleman Wheeler lived the kind of life to which I once aspired. He really did live the dream. He knew leaders from every ilk. If there was a connection to our alternate world, he knew someone. He is a kind, empathetic, tolerant soul. I met him while he was meditating on a park bench. He knew what I was looking for and where I could find it. And he was right. It changed my life. I love you for all your wonder, your wisdom and your friendship.

I believe there are no coincidences in life. I needed a friend, a mentor and a guide at a crossroads in my life. A tall bearded man who lived in a zoo and built a windmill, was that being. I have no doubt he was my angel. He was wise, and kind and knew when I needed a few words to get me by. John Kanaar and his wife Rita showed me love and an understanding of people and our world I will always cherish. John died way to young but he achieved oh so much.

The music of the 60's inspired me and still sustains me. Bob Dylan is still my Muse.

Without NBC TV News in Erie, I would have missed a lot of the 60's and grew up with a different story. CKLW Windsor and WLS in Chicago brought me the music. The University of Guelph brought me the community.

My last dedication is to my lake. Without Lake Erie and Long Point, I would not have had anyone to talk to during the lonely, confusing times and the times of jubilation.

Thank you, all. You are all in this book. Don't worry. I treated you well.

Prologue

The 1960's were a turbulent time and they were my formative years. I watched the assassination of J. F. Kennedy, Martin Luther King and Robert Kennedy. I watched the civil rights marches and the riots in many American cities. I watched the Vietnam war from my living room. I watched students struck down by national guard troops at Ohio State University. I watched our climate being raped by big corporations promoting consumption and greed. I watched governments suppressing student demonstrations against the Vietnam war, racial prejudice and many other inequalities.

The music of those years gave me hope and a sense of unity against a society which had lost its humanity. I grew my hair and defined myself with bellbottom jeans, tie-dyed shirts and war surplus jackets. The peace sign became the symbol of my generation, at least for some of us. Friends went to jail for possessing marijuana. Paranoia of being arrested was very real and haunted us for a long time. And we were white.

In 1968, policemen tear-gassed, clubbed and arrested young, idealistic protesters at the Democratic National Convention in Chicago. My dreams of attaining social justice, protecting our environment and just being kind to one another were on life support. Landing on the moon in 1969 gave us one small step for mankind. Woodstock, three days of peace, love and music reassured me that I was not alone. The anti-war march in San Francisco gave me heart. I watched many in my generation join communes and experiment with alternative lifestyles. I searched for meaning in eastern religions as our western religions became social clubs and empty shells of ritual. I hitchhiked and drove across America and Canada in my Econoline van. I found a 'family' of people who cared for one other. I belonged to a conspiracy 'that did not exist.' We were all searching for peace, and we did no harm.

In the 1960's we did our own thing—collectively. The spirit said idealistically 'we are all in this together.' What each of us did mattered to the rest of us. Unfortunately, what we found was unsustainable. The dreams were put away for what is called 'reality.' Bob Dylan said many years ago: 'It's easy to see without looking too far that nothing is really sacred.'

Fifty years later, not much has changed except that the climate is now on life support. Social, economic, and racial justice are still unattainable, but sometimes there is still a glimmer of those elusive dreams. I have written here about a young generation of idealists in a new world, because I believe they will be our only hope for the future. In the 1960's a young, idealistic generation dreamed of radical change achieved with tolerance and love. That kind of dream is needed now. Peace.

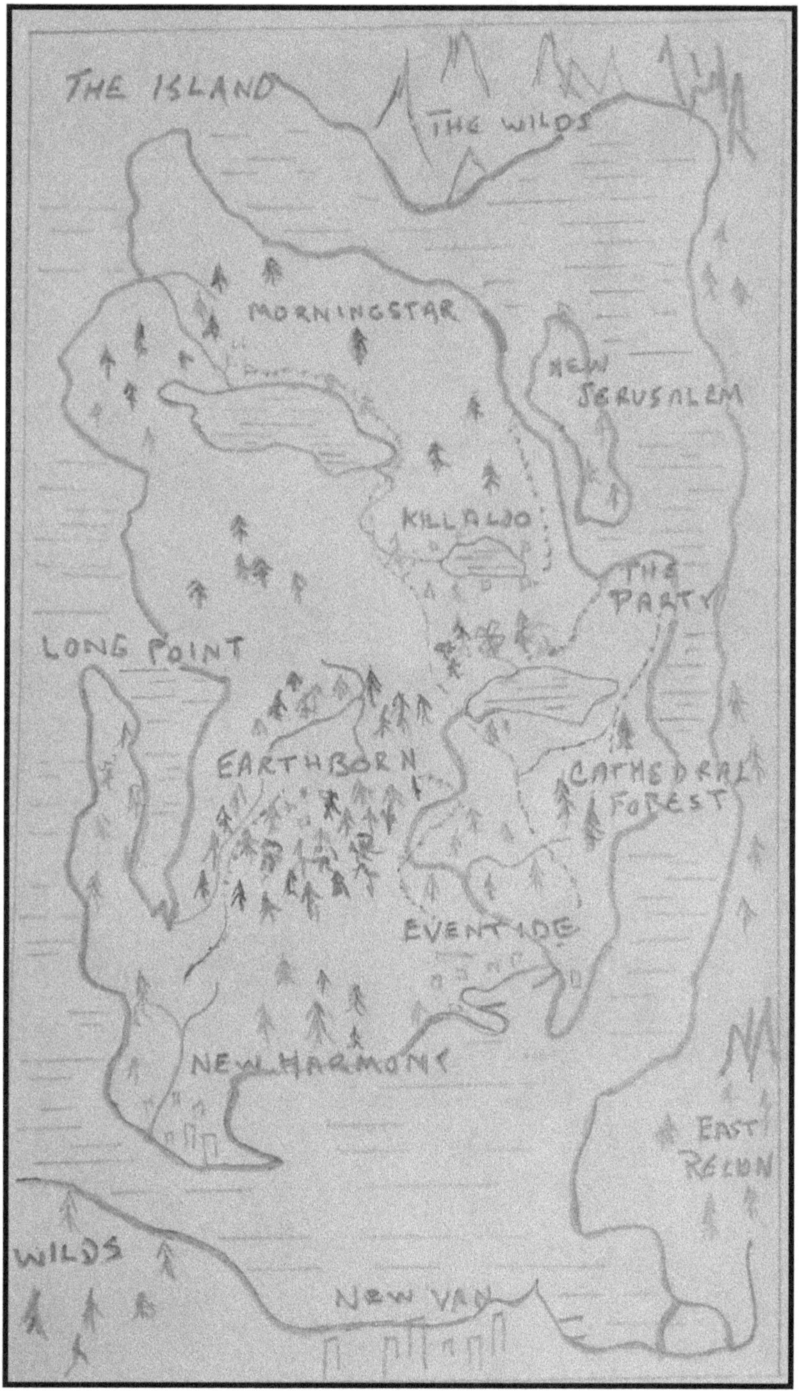
THE ISLAND
THE WILDS
MORNINGSTAR
NEW JERUSALEM
KILLALOO
THE PARTY
LONG POINT
EARTHBORN
CATHEDRAL FOREST
EVENTIDE
NEW HARMONY
EAST REGION
WILDS
NEW VAN

PART 1:

The Times, They are a Changing

I know not how I may seem to others,
but to myself I am but a small child
wandering upon the vast shores of knowledge,
every now and then finding a small pebble
to content myself.

Plato (427-347 B.C.)

Earthborn: The Day Begins

Waking was such a wonderful feeling. The sun was rising in the eastern sky. The clouds were puffed and but a few. Blue sky in the morning, a sign of a beautiful day. There were no surprises here, but there was joy and peace and expectations of a good day to come. It was the beginning of spring. He stood before the window, saw the robin get the worm and cried, "Hello world, here I come."

And so, Charles began his morning routine. Washing was a treat as he felt the warm water on his back. He dried himself in the morning sun and dressed in the clothes he laid out the night before. Breakfast was taken with friends in the common kitchen of the village hall. Going to work was as simple as choosing the activities he felt would be most fulfilling that day or performing duties he knew needed doing. Charles was twenty-three and the world seemed to be as good as it could get.

I guess he knew somewhere in his mind that this was not the way it had always been. The little knowledge he had of a different world was not disturbing, but it did arouse his curiosity. And so, he sometimes spent his time looking for evidence of the past. It was on such a day that he came upon a book. It was newer than he was used to, and it seemed odd to the touch. Books were not uncommon by any account, but this book was different. Upon opening the cover, he read the inscription there: 'Whoever sees this written word, be aware, for when what is past and what is to come takes precedence over what is now, your world will change.' He closed the book and sat on the bench under his favourite maple tree. Almost tentatively, he reopened the book. The inscription read and he spoke it aloud: "Whoever sees this written word, be aware, for when what is past and what is to come takes precedence over what is now, your world will change."

Charles' world, the village of Earthborn, was an easy place to navigate. Life was not simple and easy, but it was fulfilling and meaningful. Although there were not many villagers, growing food was a common activity for most inhabitants. The climate was hospitable for the most part, and building homes was a community activity when needed. From town centre, one could see the well-kept fields carefully planted to ensure fertility for any foreseeable future. Along the street were shops housing a multitude of trades essential to the needs of this small community. The medical centre was right beside the library and the music hall was across the street. In this community, artists and musicians were highly valued. Medical knowledge was advanced but limited to a few fundamental principles. By the stream, a fine stone mill made the finest flour. The orchard was a favourite place to visit at harvest time. Of course, the town hall was the centrepiece and all else grew around it.

For Charles, his most enjoyable activity was exploring his world after he had fulfilled his duties for the community. He roamed the fields and investigated the strange relics of a world of which he and no one alive had any knowledge. He and his friends enjoyed the times when something new was added to their world. And so it was when Charles sat down for their afternoon discussions and presented the book. "I have found something very interesting," he intoned. "I waited for you, Isla and Robert. Look at this," said Charles.

Isla was a gentle soul and eager to enjoy what life had to offer. She was two years younger than Charles and her green eyes had depth and her long flowing hair made her a vision to behold—and Charles beheld. "What have you found that is so mysterious," Isla said as she smiled in excitement. Robert, who admired Charles and was just twenty years old, was content to wait for Charles to reveal his treasure.

Charles opened the cover and read the words, "Whoever sees this written word, be aware, for when what is past and what is to come takes precedence over what is now, your world will change."

"What do you suppose that means?" queried Robert. "We do not have any evidence of a past different from now and I have never thought of a future any different than we know. Where did you find this book?"

For a moment the world stopped, and Charles thought about the question. "It was just there," he said. "It appeared on the bench near the maple over there. I picked it up." He paused, "I opened it and I saw the writing." Charles held the book as if it suddenly was of importance. They laughed and talked awhile longer and, for the moment, decided to wait and read a chapter at a time. It would be fun and would be another highlight for each new day.

There was meaning in his world. There was a certain rhythm and process. Children were being born and grew from youth to old age. Relationships were real and limited only to one's tolerance and understanding of pleasure and contentment. Sickness and death were real but just another part of the heartbeat of life. There were no weapons. There seemed to be only one rule and it was simple: care for one another and do no harm. Not everyone followed the code, and some moved on because it was too much for them to agree to. Wherever 'on' was?

The citizens of Earthborn were not alone in nature. There were many forms of animals and birds and reptiles and bugs and spiders. There was room for all. As they ate mostly vegetables and fish it was often easy to commune with nature in its many forms. There was caution, of course, and perhaps fear at times, but tempered by the rule, 'Be Kind to one another and Do No Harm.'

There was knowledge, but little high technology. Charles' society was quite advanced by some standards and perhaps quite backward by others, if you had the standards to measure it by... and they didn't. There were libraries and schools. There was communication: talking, showing, explaining, and teaching by passing on knowledge and perhaps wisdom from one to another. There were books, as well, but there was little mention of the past. Life was meaningful, rewarding, and good.

It was the following day that Charles, Isla, Robert and now a few other curious friends gathered to read the first chapter. Charles turned the first page and began,

> "This testament is written to warn future generations of the pitfalls of humanity gone wrong. Over the centuries, humans amassed vast knowledge of themselves and the world in which they lived. Lifespans grew and humankind multiplied and conquered the obstacles in its way. But there was no simple rule, 'Do no harm.'
>
> There were scientists and engineers, as they were called, who studied nature. They revealed amazing knowledge about our planet, and our relationship to it. They studied how our lives intersected with the rest of nature's wonders. But they could not protect the planet from being damaged. Often what they learned only caused more damage.
>
> There was what humanity called religions. Men, mostly, spoke to gods who told them how to live. Over time these men became the source of wisdom to millions of people. They were powerful and had books to explain the answers to our existence and how we must follow their scriptures. They had no use for scientists. As their power grew, these religions encouraged their people to grow in numbers and to compete with other religions. Over time, the planet grew crowded.
>
> It was the philosophers and writers and artists and others who strove to find order and meaning in the universe. They spoke of equality and peace with one another and nature. In

short, they sought an existence for all which had meaning and some sense of happiness and good.

There were the oligarchs who followed no doctrine at all and whose goal it was to amass power and wealth by whatever means necessary. Science and religion were theirs to manipulate to their own gains. The world organized itself in groups, and governments were formed to rule the people. But the wealthy and the powerful soon manipulated these groups as well. The oligarchs prospered and over time amassed the majority of the world's wealth. This left a large number who had very little. This was the mass of civilization who for the most part wished only to survive and possibly prosper on occasion. They were plentiful and easy to manipulate. They were not stupid, but they were often ignorant of the truth. They were most often unable to change what was, even if they knew it was wrong, even if they knew it caused harm. The oligarchs made the world work like a game and then rigged it so they could not lose."

Charles closed the book and looked at his friends who had gathered round. At first, he did not speak and then he whispered, "Do you think this world ever existed? What is this I have just read?" There was silence.

Then a younger member of the group asked, "Are we the oligarchs?"

There was a murmur among the group and Isla said, "No we are not. It is not our world, little one, but I do wonder whose world it was." The sun was waning, and it was time to prepare supper. The group split up and wandered back in smaller groups to ponder and to talk of other things. All was well with the world... almost.

Time passed and the community did what it had always done. There was joy and sometimes sorrow. Groups met to share their meals, to work in the fields, to raise their young, treat their sick and mourn those who died. They gathered to sing and to talk and to dance. And for some, there was the book.

Charles and his friends still gathered, but they did not open the book. Only Charles held the book. Others were curious but it was almost as if the book was literally out of place.

Isla spoke first. She said, "Continue reading, Charles." Clouds passed over the sun and a chill ran through the crowd. It was a pleasant day and slight changes in the weather were quite common. The expression, 'wait a few minutes and it will change' was a familiar refrain.

Charles hesitated and then opened the book to Chapter 2. He almost whispered, "Yes." And he read,

> "For centuries, humans shared the wonders of creation. They were not kind to nature, but for a time were not numerous enough to destroy their home. In time that changed. Men killed men by the millions with weapons which were capable of mass destruction. In the process, the wealth of nations was spent on better weapons and the masses grew poorer. The oligarchs amassed great power, wealth, and influence.
>
> Scientists warned of the destruction to the oceans, the decimation of the forests and the pollution of the water and the air. But they also learned how to achieve this desolation at increasingly faster rates. Poets and musicians, writers and people of knowledge and integrity tried to inform humanity of its peril. Religions did not. Religions persisted in their dogmatic rhetoric. Humanity grew as they were encouraged to reproduce and to consider death as abnormal and no longer part of the natural process. Medicine and technology lengthened lifespans by decades. Humanity's numbers grew.

> This did not occur overnight. Life was still good for nations gifted with vast natural resources. Parts of the world experienced drought and flooding, fire and pestilence and war, as wealthy nations provided weapons to make existence even more difficult.
>
> In nations around the world new belief systems grew. They preached that God gifted those who worshipped him and those who suffered obviously deserved their fate. It assured its followers that God approved of the excessive use of natural resources and the exploitation of 'lesser beings.
>
> The oligarchs encouraged this view and had the resources to be heard. They now had total control; at least it seemed that way. But the time would come when the earth could no longer sustain humanity's abuses. Nature began to fight back."

As the day was waning, Charles closed the book. Isla, Robert and now the twins drew closer. Mary and her sister, Star, spoke almost at once, "I cannot believe what you read. This is not a fairy tale. If so, do you suppose it has a lesson?" Mary and Star grew up on stories. Many of life's lessons were taught through storytelling and games.

"We don't know what it is children. We don't know why it is here." Isla intoned.

Charles smiled, "Tomorrow we will read again. If for no other reason than to hope we find a few answers to our questions."

The community was small—a few hundred souls. There were elders who had knowledge. They were well thought of in the community. However, they were not considered above anyone else. They did not control anyone, as was described in the book. They did not have more than anyone else. Robert and Isla were taking their turn hoeing the gardens and Robert stopped and raised his head, "Do you think we will ever have leaders or governments or people who have more than others?"

Isla frowned, "I hope not Robert. We have our problems, but we work together to find solutions. I like our life and I love our people, all of them."

It was at that moment that Charles arrived with concern written across his face. He whispered, "The book is gone. I cannot find it anywhere."

"But who would take it? Our friends who listen seem afraid to even look at it let alone touch it. The younger ones are content to listen to the story." Robert suggested.

Robert added, "Elder Tom was surprised when I told him what we found. He asked if we had found any other interesting relics. I told him no and he seemed to consider it of mild interest at best. We must find it though. I think it might be important. I have no idea why."

The group assembled the next day and Charles informed them of the situation. All were excited to begin the search. The twins even suggested that maybe the fairies took it, or the ogres under the bridge. They all laughed as they recalled how real those old tales once seemed. In the days following, Charles and the others found no evidence concerning the book.

Then Tom, the elder, a gentle man perhaps in his sixties, approached Charles and asked him to join him away from the others. The conversation began innocently enough with talk of friends and general gossip. Then Tom asked a question, "Where did you find the book?"

Charles did not immediately respond. Then in almost a stumble he answered, "The one we are looking for?"

Quietly Tom responded "Yes, the one you have been reading to the others. I have it here." Tom lifted it in his hand.

Excitedly Charles spouted out, "You found it. It is a most curious book. I didn't want to lose it. We have only just begun to read its strange words." In that moment, Charles saw Tom's expression change. Tom was Charles' senior and Charles respected him greatly, but he had never looked upon him as his leader. Something had changed. "What is it Tom? What do you wish to tell me?"

In that moment Charles realized they were alone and it was quiet. Tom looked into Charles' eyes and almost whispered, "What you have found I fear should never have been revealed. There are things in this book that are known only by the oldest of our colony. They could change all that we have built and the life that we now know." He paused and took Charles' hand. "In this book there are secrets that must be protected and not brought to light."

"What of the others? What shall we tell them?" asked Charles. "They are trusted friends and fellow citizens."

Others were approaching them to see what was so serious and to visit and talk. Tom again looked at Charles and said, "For now we should keep it to ourselves. I must think on how to proceed. You can do the same." With that, smiles returned to their faces and the group who had gathered were left unaware of what was said. But Charles was afraid perhaps for the first real time in his life. Isla could feel a change in Charles. Robert was perceptive enough to know there was a secret to be uncovered. Mary, one of the twins, just wanted to hear some more of the story. Already their world had changed.

The next day Charles sought out Tom. 'He must know what the book says,' thought Charles, 'He must have read it.' As he looked for his friend, he began to realize that something could be expected of him. He began to think that perhaps he was chosen to find the book for a reason. Why that would be, he had no idea. "Tom would know," thought Charles.

Down by the river in a secluded spot, Charles found Tom with the book in his hands. It was not open. Tom was a wise man according to most, and was not quick to act or judge. He expected no more of others than he expected of himself. For the most part he was cheerful and ready to see the bright side of any situation. Charles could tell that the man he thought he knew was more than he had thought him to be. As Charles approached, he stated, "I must speak with you, Tom. There is much I need to know. You have many things to tell me. I can feel it in my bones."

"Sit," said Tom. "I was expecting to see you. I have been aware of this book for many years. The book does not come from here, Charles. It comes from a place and reveals a time of which only I and a handful of others have knowledge. We hoped never to have to think of its origin again in our lifetimes. Its presence here can only mean one thing. Our community is at risk. Our world as we know it will be altered."

"Our world, our community? There are others? How many others are there?" asked Charles. Thinking there might be more was one thing. Finding out that there were, was an entirely different reality. Charles slumped to the ground. His eyes met Tom's and then they fell on the book. "What is this relic you have in your hands? Don't hide it from me any longer."

"It should not be hidden," a new voice spoke. There before them was a rather wild looking young woman dressed in attire unfamiliar to Charles. "I have come a long way and watched your people for many months. You have been chosen to perform a vital task. This book was brought to you, Charles. Not your friend. It is for you to decide what will come of it." She paused, took the book from Tom and put it in Charles' hands. "This is not your quest, Tom, but you will have a major roll to play, I am sure." With that, she sat before them as if she had been there all along. "Manners would suggest that I be offered a seat as my journey has been long, but lacking that, I will sit anyways. Good morning! I am Angela; one name and a good one."

Charles' eyes grew very large and full of awe, and then he could not help but laugh. "Good morning! I'm Charles, as you already know, and you are very strange indeed. And please be seated."

"You think I am strange. You have not been out in the big world. You and your friends are perhaps the strangest beings I have ever experienced," said Angela, with a twinkle Charles could not miss.

Needless to say, Tom was speechless through this whole conversation. Now that there was a loll, he thought he should say something. Angela beat him to it. "It's okay, Tom. We will all be friends and I will allay your fears of me, if not those of which I have to tell."

With that, Tom simply said, "That would be good."

As the day drew on, Angela revealed many things. The big question to be answered was who should have access to the book. Angela argued, "I brought the book to you, Charles, for many reasons. You are content with your life and yet still open to new ideas. You have never taken charge and yet you are looked up to by your peers. Your community has prospered, while many others have not. Its nature has facilitated this reality. Your people believe in equality for all. Your people share their resources with one another. Your people have found a balance with nature. When, why, and how this community came to be should not be a secret. It should be known by you and yours and it needs to be known by the rest of our world."

Angela adjusted her position on the ground and pointed to the book. She said, "This book was written to preserve the memory of the follies of the past, in the hope that the future would be different. Your future is different. For these reasons I believe the book should be read by all who wish to read it. It has been said that history repeats itself. It is hoped this time we can get it right."

As Charles already knew, Tom felt somewhat differently. Tom spoke up, "Our community has grown out of a very dark past.

Whether it be because it is our nature or because of circumstances beyond our knowing matters not. Our ancestors created and destroyed our world. This little place on the planet has grown from a bleak beginning to become the wonderful place that you have described. Our isolation has allowed us to grow and prosper. What was left of the outside world has left us alone. Perhaps it is best not to know of what we are capable. Perhaps it is enough to know what we know and leave the past in the distant past. Perhaps what we have is partially because we have forgotten what needs to be forgotten."

Charles listened intently, and when Tom concluded he simply said, "It appears to me that the past has already caught us up, whether we like it or not. It is also evident to me that we will each have a role to play as this new world unfolds."

In the following days, Charles spent most of his time listening to Angela relate her story. The rest of his time was spent reading the book. It was agreed that there was no precedent for hiding information and the book would be available to be read. Robert and Isla had first dibs and the twins insisted they be read to on occasion. Tom reluctantly agreed to be historian for this merry band of explorers. Public readings, with Tom present to answer questions, were of interest to many. Some did not wish to listen.

As the days passed, Angela found Earthborn to be quite to her liking. She found her dwelling to be cozy and the bed soft. The food was very good and plentiful. The people were good and kind and welcoming, and she rather liked her new companion.

Charles found his new world to be quite fascinating, and certainly a little frightening and overwhelming. It was also somewhat confusing when it came to this new girl, Angela. The stories Angela related about her life and the places she had seen were hard to believe. Yet she insisted they were real.

At dinner, Angela found it difficult to eat as question after question poured from her new companions. Isla asked, "Is it not lonely travelling on your own?" She paused. "I need my friends."

Angela responded, "This life is all I have ever known. Fear and loneliness are just small parts of it." She added, "There have been many good things as well. The world out there is different, but there is good and there is bad. I am here because we need you. You can help to make things better."

Somewhat shocked by Angela's response, Isla asked, "What could we possibly do to help you?"

Robert jumped in, "We could be an example. We could be an alternative."

"It is what I hope, but I am just a messenger. There are others you need to meet. I am asking a lot. There are no guarantees or even plans, just hope for a future that offers a good life for you and for others," Angela said with a tone of sadness beneath her breath.

Charles entered the conversation on a lighter note. "We are sharing a fine dinner with good friends. We are all thankful for what we have. Next steps are for tomorrow." With those words the others smiled.

Dinner was shared and the sun passed beneath the hills. "Dance with me, Robert, and let us make music and fun and enjoy our togetherness," said Isla. Into the night, musicians played music to rouse the spirits. The sky was full of stars and the breeze light and warm.

Charles touched Angela's hand and felt her light response, "I am glad you have come to us. We will find the answers you seek, and we will do it together."

Isla added, "We will do it together—all of us. As we have always done. It is what makes us happy. It is what makes us strong." They smiled that smile of agreement with a hint of sadness for what may already have been lost.

In the east, a new sun was rising. A gentle rain just before dawn left the world with a freshness one could smell. Charles stood on the porch and watched the robin get the worm and the man in the moon disappear. He spread his arms, looked up and cried, "Hello world. It is a beautiful day, and all is well!" It was, even if he was a bit hesitant.

Tom joined Charles for breakfast. It was decided that Angela would escort them into her world. The plan was simple. In fact, it was no plan at all. Plans had not been high on this community's agenda until now. It was agreed that Tom would stay behind, and the group of merry explorers would remain small.

At the evening gathering, Tom read a chapter in the book and then Charles asked for their attention. He said, "As you know, there is a bigger world out there. You also have read of a world before the one we now inhabit. I have been asked to tell those who will listen about the world we live in here—the world of Earthborn. Angela was sent to find us. I am going with her and ask you now whether anyone here wishes to come. There could be danger and hardship, and maybe more." The gathering was quiet. Even the birds seemed to know this was a sacred time. A time of change and decision had come.

A hand rose in the quiet and Isla answered, "I will go. I love my village and I love all of you. We have a story to tell and I would like to be there to tell it."

"If Isla is going, so are we," burst out the twins.

Robert smiled and hugged them both. "You two need to stay here and look after your family and our friends. So, I will make you a deal. I will go, and when I return, I will tell you all about our journeys. Maybe I will write a fairy tale as well." With that, Mary and Star smiled too.

So, the merry explorers were formed. Preparations were made. Dried fruit and vegetables were packed. Smoked fish was the specialty. Water was not an issue in Earthborn. It was fresh and safe from the shallow wells that fed the village. However, fresh water might be needed on the journey.

By this time, several copies of the book were made and distributed and a few would be taken with them. Many had read the book. Charles still could not fathom that it was based on reality.

Island Trails: Country Roads

Reality checked in and the merry band gathered in the square with a donkey named Carrot, and horses for each of the travellers. With goodbyes to family and everyone else, they began their trek. Angela led the way. She had prepared a makeshift map, but she knew where she was going. As the day wore on, the group began to converse with one another. Initially, it was quiet as each member took in their new surroundings. It was not so different from their home, but it was new. Woods with tall trees and meadows lay before them. There were birds and deer and rabbits and so much wildlife to see and admire. The trail was there but not well-travelled.

"Of what your book speaks has no reality here," said Robert. "It must have been a world of times long gone."

"I'm sure it was, Robert, but as we have read, the changes happened over a long timespan, by human reckoning," answered Angela. "You will meet others who did not forget the follies of the past and still live some of them. The world will change as we leave this land."

As the sun began to set, the group sought a resting place for the night. Angela suggested a fire was needed to protect them from intruders in the woods and to prepare some supper for the hungry travellers. After a fine dinner of soup and smoked fish, they spread their bedrolls and settled in for the night. Charles stoked the fire. Good nights were spoken by all in deep appreciation for their company.

By mid morning of the third day the travellers had already travelled many miles. They had forded two streams and one river and followed a well-worn path through a rather dense forest of grand cedars and pines. As they came out of the forest what lay before them was not to be believed. Before them was a vast ocean of water as far as one could see. There, a few leagues northeast, lay a town of houses, and by the water, large boats at dock and others moored in the bay.

Angela called a halt. "You see, my friends, you live on an island—a very large island, but an island all the same. The town down there is very different from Earthborn. We will ride for Eventide, but not until tomorrow. I have friends there eager to make your acquaintance."

That night, Charles read from the book,

> "Chapter 3. The signs were there for all to see if they chose to look. Nature was dying. First, humans depleted the oceans of life. The fisheries collapsed, but the oligarchs still lived well. Then the great forests were depleted and were ravaged by fire, drought and disease. The currents in the oceans changed direction and cold became hot, and what once grew in one place no longer survived. The ice melted at the poles and the oceans rose. Some coastal cities disappeared. Millions upon millions of people lost their homes and their livelihoods. Wars displaced even more of humanity. Many tried to help those who had nothing, but most chose to protect themselves. And the oligarchs did very well.
>
> Then came the equalizer. Disease had always haunted humanity, but advances in medicine extended life and conquered most diseases—at least for some. Until the viruses began. The first few were contained, and, by all accounts, beaten. But humans were not content. They created new viruses in the name of security and fear that their enemies would use viruses against them. Antidotes were found, but playing god had its flaws. Then in the twenty-first century a new virus attacked the entire planet. Humanity's economic systems collapsed. The glues that kept the oligarchs in power eroded, and the inequities of an evil, greedy system

were revealed. Over the next fifty years, the oligarchs fought to retain their power, but the planet was overpopulated, and the status quo could not be sustained. Finally, the last of many viruses and natural disasters overtook the planet. The future was left to those few who survived."

Isla lay beside Angela and nudged her gently, "How many survived?"

Angela whispered back, "I do not know. I do know that this port before us is one of the largest on the island now."

Isla asked, "Have they read the book?"

"Most have not, but there are a few who search for answers and ways to learn from our past," said Angela. "You will learn more tomorrow." She grasped Isla's hand and said, "Goodnight." In the distance, Isla could see the town. It was unlike anything she had known.

As the sun rose to a new day, Charles awoke to a vision he did not expect. Before him stood a man about the same age as Charles. "Welcome to Eventide, my friend. We have been expecting you," said the figure. "It is good you travel with our friend, for otherwise you might have found misfortune." With that, he embraced Angela, who had stood by this time.

"I see you are well, Stephen. We come in peace." She burst out laughing, and assured her 'merry' group that they were not to be murdered in their beds. Not that the thought had ever crossed their minds. Charles rose, as did the others, and looked in awe at their new arrival. Charles grinned and clasped Stephen's hand. "It is so good to meet you, friend. Angela has spoken well of you."

"And you must be Charles. She has spoken well of you as well," said Stephen.

Charles immediately spoke again, "And these are Isla and Robert, my dearest friends. Isla was still speechless. Robert shook

Stephen's hand eagerly. Charles then realized what had been said. "How could Angela speak well of me? We had never met."

"I will let Angela answer that question. But not now." Stephen laughed and winked at Angela.

The wanderers washed up in a nearby stream and brought out breakfast from their meagre supplies. It tasted good and it was shared with a new acquaintance. The world had just grown bigger again.

"The others are eager to meet you. They wait in Eventide. I thought it would be best to meet you first. There are things you need to know and rules that must be followed." Stephen began. They gathered on the rise overlooking the city. They watched it come to life. Great ships began to move. The docks were busy with people moving barrels and stacks of lumber. The hustle and bustle could be heard from where they sat. The streets came alive with shopkeepers. Horse-drawn carts moved on hard packed roads.

"In Eventide, you will be asked from where you come. You are relatives and friends of mine from the mainland. Do not reveal your real home here on the island. In time you will understand why this is necessary for now. There are many good people here. There are also those who do not follow your 'do no harm' philosophy. You have been invited here because we need to reassure those who strive for a better world, that there is hope. Hope for the future." Stephen stopped and looked to Angela to finish.

"Some of the people you will meet have come from across the water. Some have come from other parts of the island," said Angela. "I don't know how to explain all of this to you. There are settlements in many places. Most are quite different from what you know. Some not so much. The world is becoming a very busy place. There were machines once that did the work and vast economies which traded the resources of the world. Those who survived used what was available to them. There was no plan for most. Just survival in a place vastly changed."

Stephen explained, "This port is here so they may fell the trees for use across the water. The greater the cities grow, the more that is required. Survival by any means is the first rule for many. But there are others who wish to build a new world...a better world. The people you will meet are the latter."

Robert spoke next, "Why have we been kept so unaware of this place and the reality before us? We have books that have given us great knowledge of how to live and thrive in our surroundings. We do not have any books that have revealed what you show us now."

"I don't have those answers for you, Robert," Angela spoke with understanding in her eyes. "I do know that you were given a wonderful gift. There are people you will meet who can answer your questions." Then she smiled and clasped Robert's hand. "But you know more today than you did yesterday."

As they gathered their belongings and prepared for the journey ahead, Isla approached Charles. "I know it to be true, Charles. We have been blessed with gifts beyond our understanding. I am so glad we have taken this quest. We have a lot to learn, but we also have a lot to teach." With that, she held Charles' hand and smiled.

Earthborn: Revelations

Having people leave Earthborn was not a common occurrence. When the merry explorers left, it was a major disturbance to the status quo. Tom and Darla, his partner, and some of the older citizens who knew some of the secrets, began to take a more prominent role in the community. There was much to tell and many questions. Earthborn was waking to its new reality.

It was decided that the people of Earthborn should know the secrets so long kept by only the oldest in their midst. For the first time in their lives the few hundred souls in Earthborn became aware that there was a much bigger world around them. For the younger folk Angela had been a very pleasant addition and her stories were new and exciting. Darla, however, could feel the new tension among the adults of this small, safe, little community. Life in Earthborn was complex. It had taken generations to find the peace and community that existed here. The past and the future had little meaning until now. Preservation of the present was important. Meetings were called and most attended. Tom read the book chapter by chapter. He revealed that there were many communities of people besides themselves.

Tom explained, "Eons ago, there were few humans left and those that remained were not all peaceful and eager or able to assist one another in their survival. However, we live on an island, somewhat isolated, where many had come to live peacefully together. There were many who did want to join together and rebuild their lives. Those who survived were immune to the last virus that inflicted the planet." Tom continued, "They had the benefits of amazing medical science and technological advances. We, too, have benefited from our ancestor's science. We have strong immunities and have been left with some of the medical knowledge of that time. We, as you are aware, have been and are living lives of relatively good health. You have not known all the knowledge that was left to us. It was decided that we needed to find another path to avoid the failures of the past. Some knowledge was better left behind."

Robert's dad interjected, "Will my son be safe in that big world?"

Tom responded, "I believe he will. None of us know what changes are coming but we will handle them as we always have."

Darla added, "There are very good people out there who have been building their new world too. It will be different than ours, but I believe they will keep them safe."

Eventide: Good Vibrations

As the sun began to set, the weary wanderers approached the town limits. Angela and Stephen knew where they were headed. The houses were close together, and the road dusty and rough. No one seemed to be about, but there were lights in the houses. They arrived at a dead end and knocked three times on the door to a house that looked much like all the others.

The door flew open and shouts of joy and expectation awaited them. "Welcome back Angela and Stephen and all of our guests. Welcome!" voices chimed in together. The travellers were introduced and given rooms to place their belongings. After washing up, the merriment began with food and wine and a million questions from all around the table.

The party went into the night. Everyone gathered there, could feel that the world was indeed a more complex place than they had imagined. Judging by the new friends met, everyone also knew there was much love to be found. The future for now seemed bright. Charles, Isla, and Robert looked at one another before they settled into sleep. They were looks of contentment and excitement for a new day to come.

Angela and her old friends took somewhat longer to settle. Angela could not answer questions fast enough about their newfound companions. The feeling among them was not so much contentment as a state of awe for the strange and wonderful folks they had just met. These new friends were quite alien to the world they were about to experience. The unanswered question was how Angela had found the settlement of Earthborn. It would remain unanswered for some time yet.

In the morning, the merry explorers prepared to experience the port of Eventide. After the second finest meal they had eaten for many days, they were excited to see the town. At first glimpse, the sheer busyness of the place was amazing. Shops were opening along the street to sell all manner of goods. People on the street were too busy to greet one another for the most part. Some appeared very well dressed in fine clothing and others appeared almost ragged. Orders were being given to workers by others who certainly seemed to be in charge. Along the shore were great wharfs and barges loaded with timber freshly cut. Fish in large barrels were being unloaded from boats with nets on their decks. Smoke came from the coal-powered ships as they prepared to cast off. Others were in the bay waiting to dock. It was awesome.

Isla perhaps explained it best, "It is not a world I would ever have imagined. We are a long way from home."

"It is a long way from what we would like to call home as well," whispered Stephen.

Back at the house the group settled into groups of two and three, and Angela, alone with her thoughts. Angela had introduced her friends from Eventide the night before. She loved them all. There was Stephen, who knew her perhaps better than anyone. He was a thinker and a dreamer. He believed in so many things—wonderful things, and he meant to see them happen. 'Best of all,' thought Angela, 'He believes in me. He cares about me and who I want to be.'

Suzanne was the older sister she never had. Suzanne was strong and sure and there when she needed her. Angela knew she was not like Suzanne. She only pretended to be strong. She needed her friends desperately.

Doug, in his thirties and the musician of the group, brought joy to them all. His partner, Sandra, came from another time. She was grounded in the earth and found comfort in the simplicity of caring for and loving those around her. And Richard. She loved them all and cherished this time with them. But this was not home for her. She had not found home yet. As tears came to her eyes, she realized that, for now, she was not alone.

Charles came and sat close beside her and wrapped his arm around her. With his finger he caught a tear. "You look beautiful when you are sad." he spoke softly. "I don't know your sadness, but I do know you give me hope and joy each time I see your smile." He kissed her cheek and looked into her eyes. "I am so glad you found us. You are part of us now, whether you like it or not." And he smiled his wonderful smile.

"Stop. I will just cry again," laughed Angela. "Let's find Douglas. He can play some tunes. I want to be cheerful and enjoy my newfound friends." She held Charles in her arms and squeezed him with all the love she felt. In the room with the fireplace blazing, the others could be found. Angela and Charles entered and Angela sang the familiar words to Doug's favourite song. "Oh, wee ride me high, tomorrow's the day my bride's gonna come, oh yah we're gonna fly, down in the easy chair." With that, she threw herself into the easy chair and pulled Charles in with her. The others gave them a knowing look, and everyone started to laugh. No one knew the origin of the song and the words were easy to learn. It was not long before everyone present were singing along.

A few days passed. Conversations became deeper and information was shared. Robert spent time with Stephen, eager to learn about his life. Stephen came from a wealthy family who lived in the city across the channel. He wanted for little and had the privilege to explore his world and to find others interested in his ideas. In the city there were places built just for learning. Stephen was a student, but he was also the heir to a timber fortune. This was a concept which fascinated Robert. Interesting enough Stephen was perhaps more fascinated by the world from which Robert came. They became fast friends. Both shared a curious nature, and both were determined to learn as much as they could about their surroundings and how to influence them.

Doug and Sandra would rise every morning and go to work. On weekends they were home. What they did was of great interest to the new guests. Doug worked in the lumber mill. He spent his days sawing huge logs into boards for shipment across the water. He explained that the job paid for his house and food and the other things he needed to live. Sandra worked in one of the clothing stores where she was a seamstress. She made clothes for people with 'money' and it, too, paid for the necessities of life. She and Doug were partners, together in their life in Eventide. Richard had worked in the mill, but he was injured by one of the great saws. He was looking for work now. Doug and Sandra were friends in his time of need. He had the extra room. Charles had gleaned this information on his daily walks with Doug and Sandra. Sandra loved her life with Doug, and both were concerned about how hard it was to make a good life. Opportunities, as they called them, were hard to find. Life was precarious, as Richard's situation revealed.

Immediately, Suzanne had taken a liking to Isla. She was different from Angela, her dear friend. Isla was a quiet soul. Her emotions ran deep, and Suzanne could feel the poet in her new acquaintance. They both liked to read and to cook. So, while preparing dinner, they often talked of the books they had read. Suzanne gave Isla a book of works by ancient philosophers. It was Suzanne's favourite, particularly the writings of Spinoza and Plotinus. She also recited some poetry written by E.E. Cummings. Isla had never heard of them or even of a world as old as the one of which these writers spoke. Suzanne spoke of a library full of ancient books. She spoke of it with love as if it was her own. A village far north of Eventide was her home. That was as much as she would reveal for the time being.

Isla disclosed that she kept a journal of her life. She showed Suzanne some excerpts from it. She also read aloud some of the stories and the poetry she had written. It revealed a life full of joy and love. Isla recognized a kindred spirit, as Suzanne showed her eagerness for more of what constituted Isla's soul.

Doug and Sandra had spent their days off visiting with the others. That night they all met in the living room and agreed that the time had come to make decisions. No-one wished for anything to change. However, there was a reason they had been brought together.

Angela began, "I was sent to find our friends from Earthborn and to bring together those of like minds. Suzanne accompanied me from her home where this book originated." Angela held the book in her hands. "We all know some of what it reveals. It is for us to determine how to go forward so that we do not follow the same path to destruction again. We have time."

Charles spoke, "Those of us from Earthborn are glad you found us. I am still wondering why we needed to be found, especially when we did not know we were lost. How we came to live so differently is still a mystery to us."

Suzanne took the book and opened it to the last chapter. She read,

> "We, who have gathered to find a way forward, have a plan. We have chosen a group of our fellow survivors to live in a new way in a place hidden from all others. This community we call 'Earthborn' will try to build a new life using what we know from others who have sought peace and love and equality for all. In every corner of the old world, there have always been those who sought to rid the world of greed and intolerance. There have always been advocates of an economic system that allowed for all to prosper. There have been many examples of communities which have tried to live in harmony with nature and their fellow human beings. Searching for peace and wishing to preserve it has always

been a goal for some. This new community will try to build an alternative to what we have known."

Angela continued, "Your home is that community." She looked at Charles. "There are those who feel it is time for us to learn from this experiment and to reveal those revelations to the world. Those who knew have just recently disclosed Earthborn's location, and I am the one they chose to bring our people together. Where we go from here is up to us."

"We are not so different from you. In fact, I think we are very much alike in many ways," Charles said.

"Yes, you are right. But how you have lived day to day is quite alien to the actual life of those we know. Your experience goes against history and our perceptions of what is or could be human behaviour," Suzanne explained.

Suzanne then changed direction. She said, "I have asked Isla to accompany me north. It is time for my people to meet our new friends,"

"I have agreed," said Isla. She was obviously excited about the plan but a little apprehensive too. "I will be fine. I want to go."

Almost immediately Robert spoke up, "I would like to stay here and have Stephen show me his world and introduce me to others here and on the mainland—if that is okay with you, Stephen?"

"It sounds like a great idea to me." said Stephen. "Have I got a world for you to meet!"

In the easy chair with Angela sitting on his lap, Charles looked like a puppy who had lost his brothers and sisters. "I'm not sure I want to see us split up in this very different place. I don't want to split up at all," he said. "And besides, what is to become of me?"

Angela kissed him on the forehead and said, "I will look after you, and my friends will take good care of your fellow explorers. I have plans for us. Trust me." She smiled and put her head on his shoulder. "Besides, I need someone to look after me." And she meant it.

Doug, Sandra, and Richard looked at one another and Doug sadly said, "It appears that they are deserting us. Was there something wrong with the food?" The mood was broken, and everyone laughed.

"You all must promise not to stay away too long," Sandra added, "And just for the record, you did most of the cooking, Doug."

Richard, in his quiet way, said, "I rather liked the food and I will miss the company." With that everyone gathered for a group hug. It was somewhat awkward but very heartfelt.

Two days later, with packs loaded, they were heading east and north. Angela and Charles were saddled on the horses from Earthborn. They would accompany Suzanne and Isla for the first stretch of the journey. Robert and Stephen planned to stay on at the house for a day or two longer, and then they would leave for the mainland.

PART 2:

Brave New Worlds

We live in a world where we have to hide to make love,
while violence is practised in broad daylight.

John Lennon

Beauty and the Beasts: On the Road Again

Following the ocean north, Charles and his three beautiful companions, Angela, Isla, and Suzanne, used a road little used but obviously very old. For the first few miles the landscape bore the evidence of trees cut, leaving many open spaces. Eventually the impact of the foresters declined, and large cedars and pines became the norm.

After three days ride, they stopped by a quiet riverbed opening onto the large sea. The journey had been tiring and long, but they had seen a span of country beautiful to behold. They made camp and gathered wood for the fire. Charles took hook and line and went back to a small lake they had passed on the way. He caught four fine trout for supper. Angela had found some berries and they had other provisions to make a magnificent feast. Suzanne and Isla removed the packs from Carrot, their donkey. While Charles was fishing, the girls found a small pond formed in the river where they removed their clothing and washed themselves with cool but refreshing water. Charles returned to the site and went looking for his travelling companions. Not far did he walk before he saw them in the water. Angela's auburn hair was long and flowing over her lithe body as she enjoyed the flow of water splashing over her beautiful frame. Suzanne was taller and she and Isla were just drying off. It was pure beauty in motion. 'I am truly blessed,' thought Charles. 'This is just too good.' Charles then tripped on a root, rolled down the hill, and found himself at the water's edge. He was speechless. Angela took his hand and raised him from the grass.

"Well, girls, our fearless provider has returned," Angela made no effort to hide her nudity. "I think we all agree that if he is going to continue to bed down beside us, he needs a bath." With that, they stripped him bare, looked him over with approval, and threw him into the water.

'Beauty and the beasts', Charles dubbed them. He was most comfortable with his beasts and he liked his new nickname. The girls were slightly less enthusiastic with theirs. That night they all snuggled close to one another beside the fire. Tomorrow they would go their separate ways. Plans were made to reassemble at Doug and Sandra's in the fall. Early the next morning, the fire was stoked, breakfast prepared, and packs carefully loaded on Carrot, who did not seem to mind.

Suzanne lifted her coffee and stood before her friends, "Here's to safe journeys and fine meetings at journey's end. I am with friends and we have a worthy mission ahead of us." They tapped their mugs and took deep swallows.

Charles and Angela, arm in arm, waved goodbye as Suzanne and Isla rode north. Shortly thereafter they, too, were mounted and on their way.

Earthborn: Origins

Back in Earthborn, Tom and a few of the other elders continued their talks. Questions were asked about the other communities on the island. Were they like Earthborn? Why had they never met them or travelled to their homes? Tom found it very difficult to articulate the answers. The information had never been meant to be revealed except to elders who would keep the secrets. There were good reasons for secrecy.

Tom began, "Earthborn was not formed by a random group of survivors, my friends. The original inhabitants of our home were carefully chosen by a group of scholars, dreamers and idealists who had studied the knowledge of the planet. They had witnessed the end of life as they knew it. This group searched for survivors who might best thrive in a world where the mistakes of the past could be avoided. The hope was that humanity might heal the flaws so deeply ingrained in our nature. In the early months after the last viral pandemic they found many who seemed to fit their plan. The Earthborn settlers would follow one sacred rule, 'be kind to one another and do no harm'. Old ways were to be left behind. All would share in each other's successes and failures. All would contribute to the prosperity of the whole. Nature would be respected as part of life. It was to be sustained. All must thrive."

In past talks, Sam had not said much, but this was of great interest to him. He was friends with Charles and Isla. He was two years younger than Robert, and his parents did not want to see him leave. At times he did wish he had chosen to join them. A bigger world seemed like an exciting idea. "Did the other villages follow this new path?" asked Sam.

"No. Sam, they could not," said Tom. "They had to live in the bigger world where such ideas were often suspect and alien. They felt they needed to be there and to build in hopes that Earthborn was a success. The oldest of our community have been aware of the folk who knew of our existence. But it was felt the secrets must be kept.

"Are Charles, Isla and Robert safe out there?" asked Sam.

"I don't know," said Tom. "We have had minimal contact with our fellow humans since Earthborn's beginning. We had to be hidden so that we might succeed. We have been many generations and many years since anyone here has left to go beyond the great woods which conceal our colony." Tom paused for a moment and then added, "Up to now barriers were kept that discouraged awareness of our existence. I am sure much has changed for our neighbours on this island. I also think that change is going to soon come to us. We are no longer hidden from the world."

From the gathering a smaller voice spoke up, "They will be safe, Sam. Isla promised me."

Mary then chimed in when her brother paused, "Robert said he would learn everything about the world out there and would come back and tell us all. He might even write a story."

Tom said, "I believe Star and Mary are right. We are strong. We have values and skills which will hold well wherever we are. Earthborn is a success. We are all a testament to this truth."

Sam, who had just turned eighteen, was old enough to know that change should not to be feared. His friends would come back, and he was eager and ready to step into this new world. In the meantime, he would continue to share with the youngsters the workings of this unique settlement. "That is the way here," he thought. As the group began to disperse, Sam was joined by his parents and two younger members of his village. Sam took the youngsters' hands—one in each of his—and said, "We have a lot to do, Raven, and you, too, Cherry. We must be ready when our wandering explorers return."

Raven's eyes were bright with the strength inherent in his name. Cherry was named after her mother's favourite fruit. Growing up with the love of her family around her, she was confident and filled with a positive nature of hope and expectations for a bright future.

Cherry gave Sam a big hug and said, "You are a good teacher, Sam, and we already know a great deal."

"A very great deal," cried Raven, "Sometimes more than our teacher." With a twinkle in his eye he let go of Sam's hand and ran ahead, expecting to be chased by his mentor and friend.

Sam yelled to his young student, "Tomorrow we go the forest. Be ready! You have a lot to learn."

Windmill Valley: The Early Morning Rain

After a day of rain, Angela and Charles stopped for the night. They had found the remains of an ancient dwelling. It was really just a shelter with a wooden roof which kept some of the rain from seeping through. They were now in country which seemed void of human settlement. Angela had led them inland for the last two days. They shared the nature around them and the comfort of friends. They laughed and teased and shared little intimacies. They had traversed several rivers, although Charles figured it was the same river crossed several times. Looking out from their shelter, they could see a small lake. It was surrounded by forest but for one meadow on the far side. Flowing from the meadow was a fast-flowing stream. Charles was sure the river was back and had just been teasing them for days.

Sitting beside one another, the two wanderers looked like a couple of drowned puppies. Everything was wet. After a few moments of feeling sorry for themselves, they decided to try and start a fire, which would be a challenge with not a dry stick for miles. Charles looked to Angela and said, "Since you are the seasoned traveller, I am sure you have a plan."

Already feeling somewhat miserable Angela shot back, "I brought you along because I was told you might have some answers. You looked bright enough."

"I do and I am," smiled Charles, "That's why I figured the least you could do is provide some dry kindling."

With that, Angela grabbed his shirt, pulled him close and kissed him with a passion Charles was not quite ready for. "Kiss me, you fool, and we won't need any kindling." Charles felt the heat rush through him. He liked this idea.

"Let's put more wood on the fire," breathed Charles. He kissed her back.

What could have been a monumental moment was quickly quashed by a sound coming from behind them. "Welcome to my valley," came a kind but solid voice. "I am John Kanaar, like the duck. I'm your host on this inhospitable day." The voice came from a tall, bearded, older man with smiling eyes. "I see you are weathering the storm in fine style. You have discovered a very interesting way of building a fire."

Charles blushed and Angela grinned. "Well met, Mr. Kanaar," she laughed, "Yes, I think it works rather well. Of course, it takes two to start the fire." She turned and smiled at Charles. Charles smiled back and shook John's hand. He was still awestruck by the kiss and amazed at the sudden appearance of 'Mr. Kanaar.' A moment later Charles recovered and said, "Well met, Mr. Kanaar. I am Charles and this is Angela and you are a great surprise."

The trail was well worn around the little lake. Not too far from the stream at the back of the meadow was a 'windmill.' Earthborn had several windmills. A large amount of power for their community came from wind power. But even so, this was a miraculous sight. Four stories high, its stone walls were topped by wood. The blades were beautiful as they turned in a regular and steady pattern, blown by a brisk breeze.

"Welcome to our home," said John as he opened the door. There awaiting them was a lady with kind eyes and an obvious warm heart. "Rita, please meet our new guests, Angela and Charles." He crossed the room and hugged his wife.

Looking at her new acquaintances, who were soaking wet and obviously very cold, she ushered them into a large room with a roaring fire in the fireplace. "My husband has a definite knack for finding interesting things in our little valley," Rita smiled and gave John a look of incredulity. "I will take care of our 'Angela' and 'Charles.'" She spoke the names aloud to be sure she had heard their names correctly. "You had best see to their horses and packs."

Angela approached the fire and looked with gratitude to Rita, "It is so nice to meet you. Thank you for taking us in. We were feeling rather desolate when Mr. Kanaar found us by the lake. We have travelled a long way, and there has been a lot of rain."

"You are most welcome here. As I said, John has a knack for finding that which needs to be found. I will get you some dry clothes and we will all have a cup of coffee. John will need a coffee after bedding the horses." Rita then left the room to find clothing for them both.

It was not long before all were gathered in comfortable chairs around the fire. Charles was wearing a thick woollen sweater and pants a little too big for his frame. Angela wore a long woollen skirt, a cotton blouse and a bright blue woollen sweater that matched her eyes. Both Rita and John wore homespun attire which made them seem very much an integral part of the room. In the background, the gentle hum of the windmill could be heard. Dim lights flickered as the electric current ebbed and flowed. Rita had brought out a platter of fruit and vegetables, nuts and fresh bread generously lathered with butter, complements of Gertrude the goat. And of course, coffee for John.

Both Angela and Charles felt this was no coincidence as they looked around the beautiful rock and wood home and the people who had found them. They had been blessed and help had come when it was needed. 'The universe is unfolding as it should,' thought Charles. "What a beautiful feeling it is," he spoke aloud without thinking.

"Yes, it is son," echoed John, "We were expecting you. We didn't know exactly when, but the word is on the wind that a time of coming together is upon us. You will stay with us awhile and we will talk of what is and what may be for us all."

Rita said, "My husband speaks the truth, but tonight we will simply enjoy each other's company. I think it is not far off before we lose our guests to sleep. You will sleep well here and wake to a fine day tomorrow." Shortly thereafter, Rita took them to their room. She bid them goodnight and returned to the great room, refreshed John's coffee, and sat close beside him. "You have done well, my husband. I like our newfound wanderers."

The next morning, Rita prepared a breakfast of hot porridge, fruit, warm bread, bacon and blackberry jam. Charles' mouth watered and he said, "Blackberry jam is my very favourite jam in the world. I would like some more, please." Everyone laughed as there was definitely more jam than bread on Charles' plate.

When everyone had had their fill, John spoke to Charles. "Come with me. It's time for my daily sojourn in the wood. It's time to commune with nature and to consider the wisdom of the ages," he laughed. Charles eagerly joined John, who by this time had told him he needn't call him Mr. Kanaar. John's border collie, Shanda, was waiting for them at the door. Charles could see as they walked that the valley John and Rita called home was occupied by all manner of birds and animals and fish in the pond, but void of any human inhabitants nearby. The windmill provided what energy they needed. John had goats and sheep and chickens. Two horses grazed in the paddock with a couple of donkeys and one shaggy highland bull. They also raised pigs. John liked bacon.

On the trail John pulled out a packet of dried weeds and put some in a wooden pipe. Charles was quite entranced by this activity. When John lit the weeds and proceeded to inhale the smoke Charles had to ask, "What on earth are you doing?"

John coughed and smiled. He said, "A bad habit of mine. I learned it when I was a kid and just could not leave it behind." Charles was by nature curious but decided for now he would forego the pleasure.

As the enchantment of the peaceful forest enveloped them, there was no need to talk. They passed the grove of blackberry bushes that had provided the jam. The mature maples to the south of them formed a strong and powerful border. Above them the sun shone on the path and the meadow ahead. As they entered the meadow, they were presented with hundreds of yellow and blue and white wildflowers. With Angela in mind, Charles picked a bouquet of the purple ones—her favourite colour.

All that was needed was a bench so that one could sit and appreciate the view, and before them on a small knoll sat a carved wooden bench just where it should be. John and Charles sat, breathed in the aroma of fresh cedar, and marvelled at their good fortune.

"I have studied the philosophers of the ages and found wisdom in their words. But none can top the wisdom to be found in the quiet of nature," said John. "In our secluded valley, Rita and I have found our peace. We tried to live in a world with people but found it to be a harsh world where the meaner nature of man often won over the kinder natures of our kind. There are many others like us. I will send you to some of them when you continue on your journeys."

"My entire life has been with people of a kinder, wiser nature," said Charles. "I can see that now as I venture into the bigger world. My community has found a way to live together and to prosper, everyone benefiting from the whole. I think it to be true."

"I suspected as much," said John. "Some of us in the 'bigger world' know a great deal more about you and your village than you know about us. We will watch over you and your friends as you bring us together again. It is your time to meet us."

Resuming their walk, Charles and John talked of experiences, small and large. As they walked, they found a bond which did not need words. It was the bond one finds in nature when made aware that, 'We are one.' Charles knew he had met a man both older and wiser than himself. He listened.

Back at the windmill Rita was teaching Angela to knit. On the evening before, Angela had marvelled at the beautiful shawl she was given to wear. When Rita revealed she had woven it, Angela was hooked. Rita was only too pleased to start her on her first scarf.

"Don't rush, dear," said Rita. "We have time. We rather like your company and we have many stories to tell before you leave our home. We also have many questions to be answered before we see you go. It is not often we have guests."

"I have been to many homes but feel that I have none to call my own," said Angela. "My life has been spent travelling between places familiar and others very new to me. I have carried messages from and to a multitude of people here on the island and most often on the mainland across the channel." Angela touched Rita's hand and said, "Your home is so welcoming. Rita you have given me a peace I have not known. Life has been hard and very tiring at times." Rita clasped the young woman's hand.

"Perhaps it is time to rest a bit," whispered Rita. "You are among friends and perhaps someday you will see 'us' as family. We would welcome that." Rita reached over and hugged Angela. A tear formed on Angela's cheek. "Now pay attention. You missed a stitch," said Rita.

Many days passed and Charles was introduced to John's world. John had spent many years on the mainland. He had learned to work with wood and stone. His knowledge of wind power came from jobs in the city and reading. He and Rita had tried many jobs in attempts to prosper. How they came to be residents here was still a mystery.

The gardens provided almost all they needed to eat. John had built winter storage for apples and potatoes and other root vegetables. They kept sheep not only for wool but for meat as well. There was of course John's pigs. A small forge had been built for John to mould metal knives and other useful machinery. A nearby source of coal provided the energy needed and there was still a source of metal objects to be found to provide the materials needed.

Rita had become quite knowledgeable of beneficial herbs and kept a well-groomed little garden full of medicinal herbs and those which provided spice to her cooking. They lived alone, but as Charles and Angela were made aware, had friends with skills they lacked.

The couple had built the windmill using an ancient stone base and then building upon it. They had lovingly borrowed from nature to build the wooden frame. The blades were a mix of wood and metal. Water came from the well only a few steps from the front door. Inside the home, everything was created by the hands of John and Rita. Created by Rita in the rainy months were woollen hangings and watercolour paintings. Made from pine and maple were hand-crafted couches, tables, and bookshelves. There were books. A grand stone fireplace centred the room, and above it was a long birch mantel.

They gathered here before the fire each evening. Above the mantel, hung on pegs in the wall, was a long metal object. One end of it, somewhat wider, was made of wood. The rest was a long barrel-shaped piece of steel. Although first distracted by the many books, Charles was taken with this item on the wall.

Charles reached up to touch it. “What is this thing?” asked Charles as he removed it from the wall and held it awkwardly in his arms. He proceeded to rest the wooden end on his shoulder and peered through a little steel vee down the barrel. It was like nothing Charles had seen before.

John took the item from Charles’ hands. “This is what is called a rifle. It is designed to kill things, most often other people. It and others like it were items many called essential in the places we have lived. I hope never to need it for that purpose again.”

Charles said, “I have no knowledge of such things.”

John replied, “We know.”

Time passed, and the time came when the travellers prepared to move on. All was packed. Maps were drawn and destinations plotted. John and Rita knew others they wanted Charles and Angela to meet along their way. Parting was hard. Promises were made to return to the windmill before winter. John and Rita waved them goodbye and returned to their home. Rita had a fresh cup of coffee brewing.

Earthborn: Lessons

In the great woods of Earthborn, Sam met with his young students. "We have many varieties of trees in our woods," explained Sam. "For us they all have different uses. The pines are best for building homes. The wood is soft and easy to use. We cut down the trees that have disease or seem to be doing less well. We never jeopardize the forest itself. This tall tree is a beech. Its bark is unique. It is one of my favourite trees." He moved on to a grove of maples. "Notice how trees grow in families. They are not unlike ourselves."

"That is a very long saw," said Raven. "I am old enough now to help."

"You are," said Sam, "And your sister will supervise our cut. Sam chose a pine squeezed between two larger ones. He explained that the young tree did not have room to grow and would better serve their community as lumber." He took his axe and notched the chosen pine. "Cherry you stand back here behind us. The tree will fall away from you." He then faced Raven, "Now you take this handle and I will take the other," directed Sam. Raven did as he was asked and the two began to move the saw back and forth, until the cut met the vee. "OK Cherry. Yell 'Timber!" called Sam. Cherry answered with vigor and Sam pushed the tree. It fell as he expected and was ready to be dragged back to the village and sawn into boards. Sam and his two helpers headed back home. Others, older and more skilled would finish the job. Sam could hear Raven explaining to his sister how important it was to choose the right tree.

The settlement's residents were busy this time of year. Spring was a time of new growth. There were gardens to prepare, homes needing work after the rainy season. Tradespeople were eager to work as the rains lessened and the sun shone. Many were uneasy after listening to Tom and others about the early trials of their village. He had begun to tell them how Earthborn came to be in a real sense. The settlers had come from many different places. They had faced many terrible situations. They had lost friends and relatives to the virus and to the chaos which followed. The island had become a refuge from a world where humans turned against each other. Fear overcame reason. Trust in each other was lost. The men and women asked to go to Earthborn were eager to begin anew. They had agreed that the whole was more important than the individual. There were to be no leaders. There was to be no money. All would share the work and the wealth with each other. Weapons would not be permitted. Perhaps most important of all was the promise to try and find ways to live in harmony with nature and one another. The basic creed was 'Be kind to one another and do no harm'.

The aims were not new concepts but were considered unrealistic and impossible by most before the Fall. After the Fall, the first members of Earthborn were committed to finding a new way to survive. Not all who first came to the village stayed. Some could not live with the reality of equality for all. A few could not recognize the benefits of working for the whole. For some, 'do no harm' required too much trust in their fellow human beings. For some, power and control were too strong a part of their genetic makeup.

The settlers Tom was speaking to now had reaped the harvest of their ancestors. They were finding ways to thrive with one another and with nature. They were thankful for a world without unnecessary violence, power, and greed. They were thankful for the bounty in their lives. They were thankful for each other. The spiritual awareness of the 'one' that joined all together was very much a reality.

Eventide: One Fine Morning

In Eventide, Stephen introduced Robert to the daily life of the busy port. First on the list of Robert's 'must knows' was the use of money. There were many new and unusual things to buy and very little was free. Robert was given a purse and some coin. Just as important was the need to keep Eventide a secret, Stephen impressed upon him.

Robert explored the streets with the innocence of a child. Some areas were not at all friendly and Stephen warned of pickpockets and thieves. Most seemed to have jobs to do and money in their pockets. A few had very little and begged on street corners. The shops had clothing of many fabrics and colours. There were familiar trades but all required money to purchase their products. There were also places to drink and to talk and meet with fellow citizens. In some places young ladies were very friendly, but as Robert found out when he stole a kiss, they were not free either. The reality of Eventide was a harsher kind of experience than he had ever known. A group of young men in working clothes stopped him on the street just outside a drinking establishment.

"You are new here, boy," said the obvious leader of the gang. "How come you by your purse. It appears quite full." He was not at all friendly and a more than a little intimidating.

Robert, with self-assurance, looked him in the eye and said, "I'm new in town, looking for friends. You look like you could help me with that. Name's Robert. Your name and those of your friends?" He lifted his hand to shake with a big smile on his face.

Rather caught by surprise by Robert's response, he shook his hand, introduced his friends and grabbed him by the shirt. They tumbled into the inn and Boris yelled, "Barkeep, a glass of your best ale for our new friend here and us of course. I don't know where he comes from, but it sure as hell is not from here."

Robert settled in for a rousing afternoon of drinks and tall stories. A few of which he told himself—but no mention of Eventide was spoken. When he was ready to leave, he walked a little funny and had been offered a job at the docks.

Boris said his goodbyes, and with authority said, "You are our newfound friend and we will have your back." And so young Robert made his way back to Douglas' with a smile on his face and a wave to all he passed.

Back at the house, he was greeted by Richard at the door. "What happened to you?" asked Richard. "Come sit down before you fall down." Robert told his story as Richard listened intently.

"You have just met the dock's most notorious enforcer. You are lucky to get out of there in one piece, let alone with money in your pocket," Richard said. Robert was not at all sure what trouble he could have been in, but all was well for the moment.

One evening when they were gathered in the big room, Stephen informed them he had to return to the city. He would leave on the ferry in two days time. He looked at Robert and asked, "Are you ready for the city my friend?"

Robert's eyes sparkled, "I am ready. Are there anymore 'need to knows' I don't know yet?"

Stephen laughed, "Well you have made friends with the meanest guy in town, so maybe we need to take some pointers from you." He paused and then continued, "The city is quite large. It is divided into several districts, each controlled by very rich men. My father is one of them. He has made a fortune providing lumber for expansion. Others control the power supply. One conglomerate controls the shipping industry. Each have 'security' to protect their interests. Some make money by controlling money much like they did before the Fall."

"How do you fit into this interesting world?" asked Robert.

"Right now, I am a student," said Stephen. "I have privileges that many do not. I and many of my acquaintances do not like the direction our fathers are leading us. We have studied the old books, read of alternatives tried and most often failed. We often meet. That is how I met Angela and she in turn expanded my circle of friends. And so, we move on in this brave new world."

New Van: Keeper of the Key

In the early morning, Stephen and Robert boarded the ferry that connected Eventide to the Mainland. High buildings could be seen from their place on deck as they approached the mainland to the east. "Many of those structures are but shells from a long past age." explained Stephen. "The people of New Van have found ways to use some of the old technology and the structures left behind. For most life has not been easy." An hour later they disembarked.

The city streets were a mix of dwellings in good condition and those which were falling down from disrepair. Many were surrounded by tall walls and barbed wire. A large vehicle which carried several people at a time moved along rails through the city streets. Stephen and Robert took the 'trolley' and stopped at a tall building on the edge of a large park. Stephen went to the door and placed a key in a slot below the handle. It clicked and the door opened.

"This will be home," he said. "I have friends here. My family lives farther down the road."

Shortly, two new faces appeared and heartily hugged their friend. Being a stranger did not stop Robert from getting a hearty welcome as well. "It is so good to see you, Stephen, and welcome friend," smiled Inga as she kissed him on the cheek. She was probably a student as well, Robert guessed. The other new face had quite long hair and was holding a guitar around his neck. Everyone was introduced and headed for the kitchen. The bags could wait. Chili was on the stove and John had just finished a new song.

"For you, Robert," said John, "You are new here and will appreciate my great talent." The others laughed and readily agreed. "It's called 'Shelter from the Storm.'" The audience listened intently to the last chord. A fine song it was, too, and very fitting for Robert's introduction to the city.

"Thank you for that," said Robert. "If you could find me a mandolin, I would love to accompany you. A harmonica would work too."

"It shall be done," said John. "These cretins will have to listen to me then." The room broke out in laughter and strong denials of John's description of his friends.

It did not take long for Robert to fit into his new quarters. People came and went from the large dorm, as they called it. Stephen had business to do with his family shortly after they arrived. He thought he would be away for a day or maybe two. With a new harmonica, Robert joined John in many songs. There were other musicians as well. Of most interest to Robert, however, were the actors in their midst. Cedric, a tall confident man, recited beautiful verse from Shakespeare. A playwright, he often mixed these finely crafted words with the songs John and his friends had written.

On many evenings, the 'house' would walk together to a two-story building a few blocks away. On one such evening Robert climbed the stairs to the cafe and entered on the second floor through the big oak door brightly painted red. In its centre was a carving of a black swan. Inside were many round tables with wooden chairs facing a makeshift stage. At the side of the stage was a wide door which opened to the kitchen. Waiters with aprons were going to the tables, almost filled, with a wide variety of patrons. Robert's new friends found a table near the stage and they all settled in, very happy to be there.

Robert felt right at home, as the atmosphere was warm and inviting. A perusal of the patrons seemed to reveal a gathering of people dressed in very different attire and of different levels of wealth and place in society. Yet they all shared a common spirit. This place, The Black Swan Café, was a 'refuge' in their city.

A young man in jeans, a blowsy shirt, and an apron with an embossed black swan arrived at their table. "Welcome all. Good to see you again. And who is your new conspirator?" he said with a smile.

"Meet Robert from the island. He washed up a few days ago with Stephen," said John. "He plays a fair harmonica, and if we can find a mandolin?"

"That is very good news and one shall be found," said the waiter. "Well met, my friend," he said as he shook his hand in a grip which grasped his arm above the hand. Orders were taken and glasses brought with ale and wine and one fruit juice for Rose.

"To Rose, the first of our family to bring new life," said a young man next to her. "When she or he arrives, God help her with this crew."

"Aw, but she will be loved," said Rose. They tapped glasses and cheered. The food soon arrived. There was stew and chili, curry dishes and plenty for all. There was little talk for some time as everyone enjoyed their meal.

What Robert had not expected came shortly after their repast. Cedric got up from the table and approached the stage. He welcomed everyone and recited a poem from 'The Merchant of Venice.' Its origin, Robert was told later. The phrase 'quality of mercy' stuck with Robert. Then Cedric was joined by his friend Richard, and a guitar for each of them. They began to sing 'Clouds so swift, rain won't lift, gate won't close and the railings froze,' and the crowd joined in with 'Oh wee ride me high, tomorrow's the day my bride's going to come...' Several songs later, Cedric invited John and Robert to the stage. The mood was electric. Robert's mandolin was a hit, and John played 'Shelter from the Storm.' Inga was most impressed with this new musician. Robert could not help but notice her face smiling up at him on the stage. She had long straight black hair and brown eyes which could melt ice. He made himself a promise to get to know her better.

The room settled into quiet table conversation after the performances. The table next to Robert's could be overheard. Mention was made of a disturbance east of New Van. The speaker was a member of district 7's militia. He was recounting how they had been sent east to quell a protest there. Timberland's crews had moved east to begin the cutting of forests there. The settlement was vehemently opposed to the desolation of their forests. The speaker was quite upset. He related that the conflict had resulted in several deaths. His militia had burned houses and left the settlement in ruin. He was in tears and said, "I didn't sign up for this. It was wrong. I am so sorry." He was then silent. The group left shortly thereafter.

Robert stored that knowledge away to be explained at another time. Other tables began to empty. His group left for the exit. At the exit door Robert noticed a large pail and above it a sign which read 'Give What You Can.' Robert looked around at his group of new friends. From them, he felt the vigour and the optimism of youth. He also recognized a strong bond, perhaps ignited by a world gone wrong. He dropped his coins in the pail and read the sign again, 'Give What You Can.'

Killaloo: Teach Your Children

On the road again, Charles and Angela were eager to meet the community the Kanaars had sent them to visit. The journey was not far and one night under the stars was welcome. Once camp was made and a fine fire stoked, they prepared some vegetable soup, beans, Rita's bread, and Gertrude the goat's fine butter. The day had been clear and no rain seemed to be on its way. As they settled for the night, they heard a noise from the bush. From the trees appeared a rather odd-looking character. He was very unkempt and certainly not a seasoned traveller.

"What do we have here," he didn't really ask but stated. "I am quite hungry, and I am sure you would share what you have." He had a small pack but offered nothing to the feast.

"You are welcome to share with us but perhaps you should introduce yourself first," said Angela in a not so friendly tone. "It is late, and we are not accustomed to strangers appearing in the night." Charles just observed as Angela took charge.

"I am harmless, relax," said the stranger as he took some soup from the pot.

"What is your name and from where do you come?" asked Angela a little more sternly.

The stranger was little affected and simply said, "I am a citizen of the world. I have many names." He took some bread and beans.

"Give us one or kindly leave us in peace," said Angela. She then gathered the pot and put the bread back in their pack.

"Not a fine welcome for a stranger," issued the stranger still chewing on some bread.

Angela responded, "Some strangers come in peace and brotherhood. Others come just to take what may be taken. I fear you may fit into the latter." She paused and then added, "Now leave us and go back to your camp. We have a long day ahead tomorrow."

The stranger at first was ready to respond but thought otherwise when looking into Angela's eyes. He picked up his pack and faded into the night. Angela then spoke to Charles, "We best have an eye this night. I do not believe he would hurt us, but I am sure he would be happy to relieve us of our packs and horses."

The night came and went without incident and the travellers packed up early, eager to see some friendly faces. Mid-morning, they came to a small cottage built below and under a rock ledge. A small windmill was twirling nearby, and a small stream ran at the edge of the clearing. As they approached, they could hear a fiddle being played. They dismounted and approached the door.

"Hello," came a deep voice from within, "Come in. Come in. The name's Barney. Sit, and I will make some tea."

"Charles and Angela," said Charles, "We have friends who sent...,".

"I know. I know." Said Barney. "I recognize your name, young lady. I have heard of your visits from others. And you, young man, we have been waiting for you for some time."

Charles was taken aback. "I seem to have a reputation," he said.

"It is a good one, my friend," said Barney.

Barney's wife Cathy was a teacher, and they were told they would meet her and their children later. They were in school. Where Charles and Angela would stay was a house down the road. A family of three lived there. Barney's house had no extra beds, but it was plenty big enough to entertain friends and catch up on the news.

Several other homes were in the vicinity. Each household was quite independent but shared in things they thought to be important. Education was at the top of their list. They taught their children the practical skills of life but also the importance of equality for all and a deep appreciation for their environment.

Music seemed to be the part of life that raised their spirits and brought them together. Barney's fiddle was a staple of Killaloo get-togethers.

Barney explained how life was becoming easier, but there were still those who lived only for themselves. The community was not isolated from the old world of fear and violence and distrust. Barney also described how they looked after each other and were determined to make a better world for their children. Care for one another and do no harm was valued here.

One evening when they were gathered at a fire in the meadow, Charles asked about the man they had met in the woods. Barney talked of other small groups and individuals who were trying to rebuild their lives. Some had come from the mainland only recently and brought deep scars left from their lives there. They held distrust and hatred for most. Their survival skills were weak. And recovery from earlier experiences would be a long road. The man they had met was just one of the lost souls who had still not found much connection to his world. But Barney was optimistic that progress was being made. He was a prime example of one who lived by example.

Charles spoke often of Earthborn. Angela had spoke of the Morningstar alliance and the Black Swan conspiracy. They were allies. She trusted these people and they needed to be introduced to Earthborn. Its location needn't be revealed. He talked of the similarities and the differences. The fact that Earthborn even existed was a still a shock to many. Charles explained how they had found ways to work together and to find solutions to human problems through building common ground. The absence of weapons, or even the history of such, had been a blessing. The fact that wealth was measured not in money and possessions but in community prosperity was probably not believed by many of his listeners. Perhaps the biggest revelation was how Earthborn had been kept a secret. Charles himself could see how blessed they had been to be able to start fresh from chaos and destruction.

Their time in Killaloo had been eye-opening for both Charles and the community. As the spring eased into summer, they knew it was time to move on. It was time to travel back. Angela had a few stops to make before arriving at Eventide. Most importantly they had promised to make another visit to John and Rita. The windmill was a must destination.

Morningstar: Do You Believe in Magic?

The journey to Morningstar had been a marvellous adventure for Isla. Along the way, Suzanne had introduced her to a myriad of characters. Most chose semi-isolation as protection from the dangers of the world after disease, climate change, and human violence. Most were glad to see Suzanne and to meet her new companion. Finally, on a June day, they arrived in a small village on a lake a few miles inland from the channel. There were many houses, all of wood, in many different colours. As Suzanne and Isla approached, it was as if the whole village came to greet them. Isla took in the scene with such joy.

Women in many coloured blouses and long skirts, and men in garments just as colourful, appeared to fill the street. There were children of all ages.

The main street had all manner of stores and places to eat. At the end of a dead-end street was a large building with the word Library above the door.

"We come bearing news from all our friends," said Suzanne. "I bring my new friend, Isla. You are going to love her instantly. She has many stories to tell."

An older face came out of the crowd. Her hair was grey and her eyes, weary, but bright. "It is so good to see you, daughter." She hugged Suzanne warmly. "Come, we'll go to the cafe and share our good fortune together. As others followed, the tables soon filled, and drinks were brought for all.

Suzanne's mother began, "Isla, it is our ancestors who first devised a plan to form Earthborn. It is our people who have kept the secret. It is us who decided it was time to meet the people we had kept secret for so long. We all look forward to hearing your story and introducing you to our world."

"I don't know what say but thank you for such a welcome." Isla continued, "I believe you will be very happy indeed to know that all who live in Earthborn deem it a wonderful place to live. As I have travelled the last few weeks, I realize how much I have to learn. It has and will be a mutual experience." She paused, "However, I have concerns for the future of Earthborn once revealed."

Emma frowned, "There was little choice but to prepare you now. The world is growing, and your secret would not long last."

Suzanne ordered food, and when the meal was finished, Suzanne, Isla, and 'Mom' walked to their home next to the library. The horses were stabled and their packs unloaded. The day turned into night, and tired but happy travellers slept with happy dreams. In the morning, after a fine breakfast and more conversation, Isla was taken to the library next door. She had never seen such a quantity of books. There was all manner of subjects. The history books were the most interesting. Although Earthborn had books, few if any were of the history before the Fall. There was also a vast collection of books that taught survival skills of every kind.

Emma began to explain, "Before the Fall, a community of sorts already existed on the island. Artists and craft persons found in each other common bonds. Wanderers, seeking peace and opportunities to live lives they imagined, found their niche in quiet places. People interested in growing things, built farms. Inventors and engineers found a place to build their ideas. Spiritualists and philosophers found their order. The island's native community was strong. Dreamers of all kinds felt the beauty in this land and found some peace. After the Fall, those who remained found one another and struggled together to survive and build a new world out of the ruins."

Isla listened intently to all she was told.

As June turned into July, Isla experienced the vibrant little village. There seemed to be an underlying ethos to life in Morningstar. Truth, that voice inside each of us that wants to speak, was welcome here. Not only was it welcome, in many ways it was demanded. Ironically, the place that created the Earthborn secret had virtually no secrets from one another.

Isla kept her journal daily. She wrote about the talented artists whose paintings and sculptures adorned the small village. She marvelled at the musicians of all ilk who performed in various venues. The homes were eccentric—if such a term applies to houses. Trees of all kinds bordered the earth and rock paths. Isla often sat in the garden where a labyrinth had been created from flat stone found in a nearby quarry. She removed her shoes and washed her feet in a small earthen basin, then walked and found the peace all souls sought but seldom found.

Early most mornings, Isla and Suzanne and many others gathered to meditate and welcome the sun. This was followed by the practice of martial arts. Most villagers were well versed in the art of self-protection. They had learned from an early age the ways to avoid or stifle violence and aggression. They also learned how to inflict harm, but hoped it would never be needed. In reality, it was just good exercise.

Suzanne and Isla rested under a large oak following their workout. Isla brought out her journal. "You are writing again, my dear friend," said Suzanne.

Isla looked up and smiled, "I have so much to write about. Your people are so warm and open. You have such a wonderful home." Then she asked, "Why even create Earthborn, do you suppose? You have found beauty here."

Suzanne had to pause. Then she said, "I only know what I have been taught and what I have read, Isla. I am much like you. My world has been kind to me, as has yours. Perhaps Earthborn came out of dreams from a people who, for a time, lost all hope. Over time, those dreams returned, as broken lives were mended and wounded souls found love again. Morningstar is perhaps the realization of old dreams restored."

"And Earthborn is the realization of new dreams not yet fully formed," said Isla. She wrote those words in her journal and closed her book. She stood and embraced Suzanne with a love which touched their souls.

Isla and Emma talked often. Emma revealed why the time had come to introduce Earthborn to the world. She explained how the communities of Morningstar and Earthborn were not alone anymore.

She said, "New Van and other cities on the mainland are growing fast. They were not based on the community spirit you and Suzanne have known. They grow out of chaos and the old pillars of power and greed. Environmental and human degradation are taking hold again. The time has come for us to try and save what has been built and to teach a better way forward.

Emma continued, "Morningstar has been, for many, a beacon. The island has been a refuge where many have come to find some sense of peace and renewal. The Morningstar Alliance has offered support in providing basic needs and skills to newcomers. Morningstar has also offered the wisdom of books and experience. It has offered comfort and solace to the weary and broken.

Emma told Isla, "The island is no longer the isolated realm which has helped so many. It is under siege from a world we hoped to leave in the past.

Isla then realized and said, "It is from here the 'Book' was written. It is you who have compiled the history."

"Yes," said Emma.

"We cannot tell you where to go next," said Isla. "Earthborn is but a little place. We have been sheltered and protected."

"This burden is not for your shoulders alone," said Emma. "We are all in this together. You are now part of a conspiracy for peace."

Suzanne joined them and took Isla's hand, "You and I have many miles to go before we rest. Together we will find our way forward. There will be so many more who will join us along the way."

Emma smiled, "We will find our way. Our numbers are growing, and our mission is worthy."

New Jerusalem: Good Times Bad Times

Charles and Angela had looked forward to being on the road again. Their packs were full and summer had not yet waned. Angela chose a different route south. She wished to stop at a small island settlement that could only be reached across water. The pilgrims, as they called themselves, had built 'New Jerusalem' after years of conflict over their religious beliefs. Charles and Angela arrived by a small barge on a warm July day. When they disembarked, they were confronted with a tall white edifice. The church of New Jerusalem stood before them.

"Welcome, Angela. Do you bring greetings from our friends on the mainland?" said an older man who seemed to be in charge.

"Hello Abraham," said Angela with a slight look of disappointment on her face. Not this trip, but I can take your mail. I do bring a friend who is eager to meet you."

"Ah, yes. Welcome young man. Are you one of God's followers?" asked Abraham, who had by then indicated that he was to be called Brother Abraham. Several others had come to join them. They did not appear to belong to a prosperous community.

Charles smiled and in his confident manner simply said, "I am pleased to meet you 'Brother Abraham.' I come in friendship."

"I am sure you do," said Abraham.

Angela stepped in and indicated, "We will need a place to sleep and some food. It has been a long trek, and we look forward to your hospitality." She waited for a response and added, "Our packs and our horses need tending."

"Of course, my child," said Abraham. He waved to a young woman beside him. "Jana will find you food and shelter for the night. Adam will take your horses." He added, "Perhaps you would first like to pray?"

Angela was about to speak when Charles spoke up. "Of course, we would. I would like to know your ways, and I will gladly listen." So it was that Charles and Angela found themselves talking to God in the large open room of the church.

The temple, as Jana called it, had been built well with much adornment and care. Charles noticed the places they called home were not quite so sturdy. They were perhaps adequate for fair weather, but would not be comfortable in the upcoming winter.

Jana's god seemed to require a fair amount of attention. Charles' interest had certainly impressed Brother Abraham. However, the brotherhood seemed to wane when Charles did not offer his life to the church.

Dinner was sparse and the accommodation somewhat wanting. The following morning, Angela and Charles rose early to a small breakfast, and eagerly prepared to leave. Abraham gave Angela some letters to take to his 'flock,' as he called them. Jana came out of the crowd and wished them well. She looked at Angela. The others just watched.

"I wish you would stay," Jana said in a whisper. "We will miss you."

Angela reached out and held her hand, "Thank you, Jana. I look forward to seeing you again." A tear may have appeared on Jana's cheek. Charles hugged her and said goodbye. Abraham turned towards the church and the others followed. Jana waved goodbye.

New Van: Bad Moon Rising

Stephen had been away several days. When he arrived back at the dorm, he seemed somewhat subdued. John, Inga, Cedric, and the others had gathered that evening for what seemed to Robert to be a meeting. Robert had heard the word 'conspiracy' used in what he thought was a joke. Perhaps it was not. The dorm living room was filled with faces he had seen at the Black Swan coffee house nights before, and others he did not know.

Stephen began, "I am so glad to see you all. I have some troubling news." He was tired and sad. "I have been to see my father, as you know. He revealed to me that there are new markets for his lumber. The forests east of us are still plentiful and my father's company has sent their militia to remove those that would prevent them from clearing them."

Robert asked, "Is that the 7th district militia?"

Stephen was aghast, "Yes, how do you know?"

Robert told everyone of the conversation he had overheard at the Black Swan. Most in the room were not surprised as much as saddened. Two young men Robert did not know stood up. They were visibly angry.

"We have waited long enough to take action," said a tall, redheaded man with longish hair and a scar across his hand. "We have friends in the east, some of whom may have been involved in this massacre. Did your father tell you how many were injured or killed?

"There were deaths, Ronald," Stephen answered. "There will be more." Stephen paused and then continued, "I confronted my father, and he assured me nothing would stop his progress—including a relationship with his son."

Cedric hugged Stephen and whispered in his ear, "Don't give up on your father. There is still time." Stephen knew he had friends here who could feel his pain.

All those gathered agreed to go back to their friends and to meet again in a month's time. Some lived a distance away and some had few resources to travel.

When the room had emptied, Robert moved his chair close to Stephen's. "What is happening here, my friend?"

Stephen sighed and said, "We live in perilous times Robert. Those who control our resources are expanding their reach. Smaller towns and villages are at risk of being destroyed as companies like my father's grow. As you have seen, some do very well. Others have little and do the bidding of the powerful."

"But there seems to be room for all, if we make it," said Robert.

"Yes, if we make it," said Stephen. "There is a movement growing to change the direction our society is moving. It is called 'The Black Swan Conspiracy.'" He laughed. "It is not as dire as it sounds. Many people like ourselves are coming together bonded by a common goal. We want what you have found, Robert, but we don't know how to get it."

They talked for many hours. Stephen told him of the 'New Life Community' where many met to celebrate life and to find ways to make it better. They would go there soon.

"But not tonight," Inga's voice whispered from the hall. "My bed is cold, and I need Robert to keep me warm." Robert was only too pleased to comply. "Goodnight, Stephen," said Inga.

"Goodnight Stephen," said Robert as they disappeared down the hall.

The Festival of Love: Celebration

The barge trip off the island was a quiet one. Neither Angela nor Charles were in high spirits. The encampment they just left was not well prepared to weather an island winter, and their expertise in basic survival seemed wanting.

In her travels, Angela had many connections. She was a lifeline to some, and to most, a welcome face from a bigger world. For the most part she would find shelter with others on her travels. She was not surprised in mid afternoon when an unusual sight appeared before them. Overlooking the sea, sitting in the lotus position on a rock, stark naked, was a very hairy man with a very wide smile.

"Well, well, well, look who comes to dinner," the voice almost sang the greeting. "Our little band of nature's children have missed you, Rosebud."

Angela's smile grew broad and she embraced her old friend with a hearty hug. "Oh Abdul, or have you changed your name again? It is so good to see you."

"Today my name is Abdul just because you are here, Rosebud," laughed Abdul. Angela quite liked her adopted name.

From out of the trees appeared another quite naked individual. She slapped him on his bottom and said, "Abdul! A fine name. Whatever happened to Raymond?"

Abdul or Raymond said, "He is alive and well and hiding under all these clothes." He then introduced his kindred spirit, Flower, and welcomed both Charles and Rosebud to their party by the sea. Flower also revealed that her city name was Barbara. She was not quite as obsessed with names as her partner.

The music and the merriment could be heard before Charles could see the incredible group of souls gathered around a large fire, cooking all manner of food and drink. A sweet smell permeated the air. It seemed to have a very positive effect on the gathering.

Some wore clothes, but the vast majority did not feel the need. The gathering of souls was quite diverse. Humanity came in many colours and shapes. And here they fit very well together. Angela distributed the letters and greetings from their friends elsewhere. She grabbed Charles' hand and they joined in the dancing and the merriment.

The event went well into the early morning hours. Abdul called it a celebration of the sun until it got dark and then it became a celebration of the moon. Charles was sure they needed neither sun nor moon to celebrate. It really was a celebration of nature and of life. As Abdul would say, "The gods of nature are in love with life today."

The next day, not early, people began to appear. A communal breakfast was prepared. Small groups formed to greet one another and the new day. Angela hugged Charles and whispered, "Thank you for being here with me."

Charles beamed and held her close, "I would not wish to be anywhere else in the world."

Abdul joined them and hailed his group of friends. He said, with a twinkle in his eye, "From this moment on I dub Charles the newcomer to be named 'Sparkle' for his unending ability to make Rosebud's eyes smile."

Charles simply said, "Thank you for this show of love. I will always think of you all as my 'lightness,' for the lightness you have put in my step. I will remember your names with great fondness." He hesitated, but then asked, "What is your fascination with names, Abdul?"

Abdul answered, "I have a name for every situation. It keeps life interesting."

With that, Marigold, Leaf, Amber, Dandelion, Oak and the others all carried their newfound friend around the circle in the welcoming ritual. 'Sparkle' was now a part of the family.

As Rosebud and Sparkle prepared to leave the next morning, Abdul and Flower first sat with them on a log facing the sea. Abdul explained to Charles that the folk who he had just met would all be returning to the city, or other settlements on and off the island, in a day or two.

Abdul said, "We gather here a few times a year to celebrate life. Our lives are not always easy. It is therapeutic to meet with like-minded friends to reaffirm our hope and optimism for the future. We welcome you, Charles, as a beacon of hope. We will all need one another in the near future."

"We will meet again soon, my friend," said Angela. "Charles has yet to see New Van, and we will come and worship at New Life Community one day. Our mission is worthy."

"So it is," laughed Abdul. "Safe journeys, Sparkle. Go with love, Rosebud."

New Life Community: Hallelujah

The big doors were wide open. The great stone edifice was filled with hundreds of bodies. Some stood. Many danced with others and themselves. A few looked to be in meditation. All were there to hear and to feel the spirit of the place and its people. This was the New Life Community everyone was talking about.

Robert, Inga, and Stephen found a seat as others moved over to make room. Up front, a speaker in colourful robes, obviously homespun, began to talk.

"We are all Children of the Universe. We are meant to be here. We all have a right to love, security and an equal place in this world with all others," said the man before them. "You have a right to be who you are. We do not judge here."

He then raised his hand, "This book reveals the history of a civilization gone wrong. Its old testament recounts the horrors experienced in the great extinction. It articulates the follies of our forefathers that led to the Fall."

Father Raymond continued, "Before the Fall, the world—the whole world—was connected by electronic communication devices: computers, as they were called. When the mega powers of electronic communication and so many other powerful corporations fell silent, chaos ruled. Communication, as the world knew it, was gone."

Robert was amazed, "He is holding our 'Book,'" he cried.

"Yes, he is. Listen. What's coming next is why we are here," said Inga.

Father Raymond then broke out into a beautiful smile. "Out of chaos, a new communication is rising—not only between human beings, but with all the wonders of creation. And a new book is being written. We are writing it. It is a revelation of how communities are growing. It is a blueprint for how people may live together in harmony. It is a book of hope for the future. We are that future. You are that future. We will find our way," he said. Then the building burst into songs of celebration and hope. People danced and clapped their hands and hugged their neighbours. Some laughed. Many sang with real joy in their hearts. Some, damaged by the world, broke down and cried.

Father Raymond, with hands outstretched, said, "We will make this journey, in love, together."

Overwhelmed by the mass of humanity around him, Robert felt the warmth of his fellow human beings all looking for connection in their troubled world.

When the band stopped playing and the last song ended, Barbara came to the stage. She was a warm and gentle soul with a fierce spirit. "Many of you are hurting and need support, and we can all help each other here. The basement is full of people and organizations ready to assist you and to build a better New Van and a better world. Go in peace." She then held her hand up with her fingers split in a vee, the sign of peace. The people responded in same. With that, the meeting ended.

Inga took Robert's hand and led him to the hall below. Dozens of tables were full of information and helpful people. Many churches served meals for the hungry and offered services for the soul. Co-operatives offered opportunities to work together to achieve new goals. Educational opportunities were available too. Organizations to help people in desperate situations were there. Some offered spiritual guidance. The desperate and the broken from the city gathered here. There were also political and activist groups, the Black Swan among them, offering hope for a better future.

Robert began to realize that the world he grew up in was very special. When you have never wanted for food or shelter, poverty has no meaning. When you have always provided for your family and always had a job, the jobless can be invisible. When you have always had access to services you need, you may be blind to the lack of services for others. When you have always had community, loneliness and isolation have no context. Poverty is mean and desperation crippling. Robert saw the effects in the eyes of those who came for help.

As he and Inga walked home hand in hand, he looked at the streets around him. There was a better way to build a world. He promised himself that he would do his part.

Days later, Robert ventured to a section of the city where, out of the ruins, houses were being restored. Gardens appeared on front porches. Outside one grey, well-kept building, there was a sign which read 'Foundation of Revelation.' He had stopped by their table in the New Life basement. They originated in a city across the channel. As fate would reckon, a young woman was sitting on the front porch.

"Welcome," she said, "We were expecting you."

"Really?" said Robert, "I was not aware I was coming here, but I am most pleased to make your acquaintance."

She smiled, "We are a small community and growing quickly. Many of us were very lost and needed a direction home. We found our home and our family here. We support one another and our only judgement is demanding the truth from others and ourselves. I am on my way to our weekly gathering. Would you like to accompany me? My name is Charlotte."

Without hesitation, Robert introduced himself and agreed to attend. As they walked, Robert felt the peace emanating from Charlotte. He knew that feeling well.

In the large room, three dozen people gathered. A speaker of older years took the floor. His presence was mesmerizing. He commanded attention in a very comforting, gentle way. He spoke of inner truth, that feeling we know to be right. He talked about the revelation of self and the power it gave everyone who drew on its strength.

He also emphasized personal responsibility in all that we do. For those who wished to build their lives, there were resources available. When one of the family prospered, she would use her resources to assist another.

But what Robert saw was a gathering of once broken souls searching for meaning in their lives and a place to call home. At the conclusion of the meeting Charlotte read:

> The journey that was never made
> Amid hopes and perils the trail was laid
> Through adventures that never took place.
>
> Mission lost in passions transient
> Seeking pleasures always in pain
> Desire-moments fettered time through space
>
> Path blazed by desires in flame
> Journey awakes to its joyous game
> Guided in darkness, now in light
> Motion becomes its own delight
>
> The end is ever in the source inscribed
> Around the circle never described
> Time and space and motion sublime
> Rhythm of Stillness signs the hymn
>
> All is yet an intense Reality
> A moment of Conscious luminosity.

Robert would share his life with them, and often returned to talk and commune with Charlotte and her community. There was hope in this city, and people who cared.

PART 3:

Turn, Turn, Turn
To Everything
there is a season,
And a time to every
purpose under heaven

Friendship
Oh, the comfort-
The inexpressible comfort of feeling safe with a person-
Having neither to weigh thoughts nor measure words,
By pouring them all right out, just the way they are,
Chaff and grain together,
Certain that a faithful hand will take and sift them,
Keep what is worth keeping,
And then with the breath of kindness
Blow the rest away.

Dinah Craik

Earthborn: Long Time Gone

The big maple in the courtyard of Earthborn had many stories to tell. It had been a good summer. The crops were progressing well. Long gone, the apple blossoms had turned to small fruit. On the face of it, the sleepy village looked the same as it had been for generations. For those who lived there, however, the world was very different.

Charles' parents often thought of their son. He was such a fine son and they missed him greatly. Sam picked up the storytelling under the great tree, but it was not the same. Mary asked almost daily when Robert would keep his promise and come home. Star played ball in the field nearby with Raven and the other children in their midst. Charles was an only child as was common. His parents often visited with Sam's mom and dad. They could see the day when their son would leave, too.

New homes completed for immigrants from New Harmony were well placed and fit into the community. The new folk, as they were referred to and probably always would be, were well received. But there were growing pains. The ways of Earthborn were long established and unfamiliar to outsiders. The new people who appeared from the south were looking for a new place to live and Earthborn invited them to stay.

Tom, the elder, spent hours under that tree telling his neighbours about their history. He tried to be reassuring about the future, but he was as unsure of it as his friends. Thankfully, Darla was more upbeat and optimistic about their coming years.

Darla began having neighbourly chats under their tree. On one such day a dozen or so souls were sipping lemonade as Darla read some letters delivered by Cody, the new wanderer.

She started, "Dear Darla, we are expecting the arrival of Suzanne and Isla within days." Darla noted these letters were a month old. “Isla will love our town of Morningstar. I know it must be hard for all of you to grasp but I believe all will be well for you. We have a vast ‘conspiracy for peace’ and we will protect what you have made.” Darla stopped and then continued, “The speaker is Emma. She is the keeper of the library and one of the scholars who compiled the book.”

“Is there any news of Robert?” asked Robert’s sister.

“I have a letter here from Sandra in Eventide. She writes that the merry explorers, as they call themselves, arrived in Eventide in early May and were welcomed by all.” Darla then skimmed and noted that Robert had crossed the channel and was now having a grand time in New Van with a friend called Stephen. He may have met a young lady as well.” That piqued everyone’s curiosity.

“And what of Charles and that pretty young wanderer Angela?” asked Sam. Darla opened another letter. She quoted, “Angela and Charles have been seen in the Killaloo area. They may have met John and Rita. If so, they will be in wonderful hands.”

“It seems our chicks have found their wings,” said Darla. “So, stop worrying and let us enjoy the bounty of our summer. The world out there has welcomed our children. We will do just fine.” She paused and smiled, “Besides they will be home in no time.” A common expression of Tom’s seemed appropriate. Darla ended her talk, quoting, “It’s a long road that doesn’t have a turn.” She added that change is always with us, and whether good or not so good, it is part of life.

Thoughts of Home: Going Back to Big Sur

One August afternoon, Robert sat with Inga in the park next door to their dorm. They had grown very close over the past weeks. School would be back in session soon and the dorm would again be full. All things must pass, and so, too, his life in New Van.

Robert began to talk, "The time has come to find my friends, Inga. It is time to go home. I miss them dearly and I feel that Earthborn needs me too."

Inga was not surprised. She said with love, "I have known that for some time now. Do you think me blind, you fool? I love you and you are not that hard to read."

"I love you, too, and I don't want to leave you," replied Robert.

Inga looked incredulous, "You couldn't leave me if you tried. You think I have invested all of this time in you just to say goodbye?"

"You mean?" Robert burst out.

"I am coming with you. I have a world to see, and," her eyes twinkled, "you need to introduce me to your parents."

Robert pulled her from the bench and swung her around and kissed her passionately.

"For all of your good qualities, you can be so dense sometimes," Inga laughed.

"You noticed," laughed Robert.

Within the week, Robert informed the others that he was leaving. No one was surprised when Inga told them she was going along to protect him.

Stephen laughed, "I think Robert may need protection from his protector."

Inga punched his shoulder and he said, "See. It proves my point."

Cedric and John would miss their new band member. Rose, who by now was quite big, made them promise to come back when the baby was born.

Stephen would accompany them to Eventide. Preparations were made to leave. Autumn was in the air. The leaves were changing.

Morningstar: Homeward Bound

The cool mornings of August could be felt in Morningstar. Isla's journal was full. She was getting quite homesick. News from the coast via messengers like Angela was not good. Perhaps the most worrying of all was the news that a city south of Earthborn may be threatened. New Harmony, a place Isla had never heard of, was being threatened by militias from New Van. In the library, she sat with Suzanne, Emma, and the bearer of the news. He was a tall young man, a wanderer, whose eyes reflected his love for adventure. He called himself Gab.

Isla asked, "This New Harmony, can you tell me where it is? I come from a place a few days ride west and north from Eventide."

"It is on the ocean channel at the most southern edge of the island," explained Gab. "I do not know of the place you speak."

Emma interjected, "You would not. It has not been put on any maps or even spoke of outside a very small circle."

Gab said, "I believe the people of New Harmony are at risk, as is the island itself."

Isla stood and stared out the window for just a moment. She said, "I must go back. Earthborn must be warned. Please, Suzanne, will you accompany me to Eventide and then to my home?"

Gab stood beside her. He immediately replied, "Suzanne and I will accompany you and we will meet others in Eventide." He tried to reassure her, "The news I bring is being spread to all those who are listening. Angela and I are only two of many who carry messages across this land."

Another voice came from the room. It came from a small, older woman, with greyish hair and warm eyes. Her inner strength could be felt in the room. "I will be coming as well. The time is coming for us to act and I have skills which I am sure will be needed," she said. Starhawk was her name.

Isla smiled a thank you and Gab seemed to smile as well.

Cathedral Forest: Stardust

The time had come to return to Eventide. Summer was ebbing and Angela had delivered her greetings and mail to the myriad of people along the way. Eventide was not far, and Doug and Sandra were expecting them. For Angela, this was and had been her life. The difference now was Charles. He had touched her heart. He made her think that home could be a real place. He made her feel like she belonged to someone, and even more important, that someone belonged to her.

Charles often thought about his home and the two travellers he had been separated from a few months ago. He missed the comfort and security and the love his community had to offer. He marvelled at how blessed he was. But most often now he marvelled at the woman he had come to know on their travels across the land. She had come to him in Earthborn as rather an odd creature, full of life and spark and curiosity. She was not open and deep like Isla, his first experience with a woman beyond childhood games. She expressed love and warmth, but had a certain restraint which only made Charles more eager to know his companion better.

Angela interrupted his musings. She said, "Charles, we are near a place native elders call sacred. I call it my Cathedral Forest. It is very old and full of beauty. Let's rest here for the night."

As they unpacked their horses and prepared to sleep beneath the stars, the spirit of the forest became more present. A small fire was kindled, and a meal of beans, vegetables and bread was prepared. Abdul had even put in a bottle of their dandelion wine. Angela had saved it in her pack these past weeks for an occasion just like this.

Together they gave thanks to Gaia, the one, for their good fortune, and to all other gods or entities who believed in love and peace. The great pines around them seemed to hold them in their limbs and the stars smiled down from above. The gentle earth was covered with the many needles dropped over the ages. They would make a soft and fragrant bed.

Charles kissed Angela softly on her lips. He then looked into her eyes and whispered, "Angela, I love you. I will give myself to you and cherish you forever. I give my promise to care for you always."

From Angela's eyes, teardrops appeared. She responded, "Charles, you are the love I did not ever hope to find. I love you. With you I know I will find my home."

They then stood before one another. Charles removed her blouse and her jeans slipped to the ground. She then unbuttoned Charles many-buttoned shirt and more quickly removed his trousers. The two embraced as their bodies came together. They fell awkwardly to the bed before them and then regained their focus. His kisses caressed her body from lips to toes. She caressed his manhood and they came together in a marriage of souls. The stars even seemed to shine brighter. The ritual lasted into the night until, tired, they both settled into a sleep blessed by the moon.

The morning came too soon. A new day dawned. "A new day it is," both partners were thinking. Angela and Charles rode together on the road to Eventide to be there by autumn.

A Turn in the Road: She's Come Undone

After several days on the trails and the ancient routes, Suzanne and her fellow companions came to a crossroads. Gab indicated the way south and told Isla to watch for a trail not too far distant that veered right into the woods. Shortly thereafter, Isla spotted the old stump Gab had mentioned, and the four travellers rode down the narrow path. It wasn't long before they were met by a young woman sitting beside a very large teepee smoking a pipe.

"Gab! Too long no see, my friend. Come sit with me. I have been alone too long," said the woman with a twinkle in her eye.

"I certainly shall, dear friend," said Gab. He dismounted his horse and nodded for the others to do the same. "Please meet 'Quiet Sue,' my friends. With me are Suzanne, Isla and someone you know very well."

Starhawk moved forward to embrace Sue, "Hello, my dear Sue. I have thought of you often and wondered how you fared." All else, including Gab, was forgotten, as the two of them entered Sue's home and found a corner to sit on plush cushions and to shut out the world for a time.

Isla looked around her new surroundings. How marvellous they were. A cistern sat not far from Sue's abode. A structure on stilts was probably a storage place for game. In the hill nearby was a door. A root cellar, Isla presumed. Of course, a small garden was there with a wooden fence to discourage the wild creatures. Sue even had a wee garden of roses still in bloom. Looking inside the teepee, a stone fireplace sat central to the vast living space. The walls were covered in quilts of many colours and fabrics. A bed filled one corner and on the bed was a cloth doll.

Suzanne and Isla did not enter, but sat on a bench fashioned from a log. The forest was all around. Gab had disappeared.

Suzanne explained, "Starhawk comes from New Van and then Eventide. She has been a source of comfort and healing for many who have found life in this world to be too much of a burden. She often says, 'my friends are many; some are weak, and some are strong.' She has spent her life helping the weak to become strong, and Quiet Sue is one such soul. Starhawk has spoken of her often."

"Does she live alone?" asked Isla.

"At times. At times not," said Suzanne. "There are others not far away. Eventide is but a day's ride and Sue, sometimes, goes to trade her quilts for flour and beans.

Not far from the teepee, Gab found what he was looking for. Sue's homestead was on higher ground, and Gab was now standing on a ridge overlooking the vast valley. In the far distance was Eventide. What he saw as well was a forest sharply severed not a few miles away. Beyond was the devastation of a forest newly felled.

The evening with Quiet Sue was indeed a treat. She lived a simple life. They talked the evening through, and Isla read some of her poetry. The cedar logs in the fireplace kept the dampness away. Sue sat close to Starhawk. Gab played his ukulele. Just before bed, Sue brought out candies she had bought in Eventide. The maple flavour was a delicacy beyond compare.

The next morning, Gab asked about the recent cutting past the ridge. Sue told of the coming of large numbers of men with new equipment, which made the felling of trees much faster. She feared her home would be no longer by the following summer. In the coming rainy months, she expected the cutting would cease. If so, there would be some reprieve.

Shortly thereafter, the band of four made their farewells and promised Sue they would do what they could to save her home and the homes of many others. Sue assured them, as well, that she and others were ready to assist in the effort. "The conspiracy is alive and well," she laughed.

Eventide: A Reunion

As the summer was coming to an end, the port of Eventide too was becoming a quieter place. The logging operations were slowing as the rainy season approached. Some fishing boats remained. Life would be harder with little work. The mill still employed a few workers until the logs ran out. Many moved back to New Van. One thing that would not change was the presence of the militia from District 7. They were there to protect the interests of their companies in New Van. Welcome, they were not.

Doug and Sandra had prepared for the slow months, and in company with the free folk they would help one another. 'Free folk' was a name adopted by those settlers who had left the city to find a life on the island. Some had recently left Eventide to live farther north as the militia took control of the port town. Some came ready to build a new life. Some just came with no plan and no real life-skills. Doug and Sandra were part of the Morningstar Alliance there to help in the transition.

Injured and unable to do manual labour Richard had to find other ways to contribute. He helped organize work crews and food distribution to the more isolated groups. Douglas had a fine folk-rock band called the 'Eventide Conspiracy,' and Richard became the first one-armed drummer on the island.

Just off the ferry, Stephen, Inga, and Robert, who lagged behind, were eager to see their friends again. The rains had not begun, and the street was still dry and a little dusty. Two blocks from Doug's house, a rough looking group of men with a prominent 7 on their chests stopped them in their tracks. "You are new here," said the biggest of the gang, "What is your business?"

Stephen, who was not accustomed to being harassed, was about to confront the bully.

"Boris, my friend," came a shout from Robert who had just caught up to the group. "It has been awhile, and I have missed you and your pals."

Boris slapped Robert on the back, a little too hard, and also expressed his happiness to see his old friend. Robert's companions were aghast and quite relieved.

"We've come to visit friends before the rains, Boris," said Robert. "I hope to see you again sometime in my travels. I think you and I have moments to share in the future."

Boris responded with a smile beneath the angry scar over his eye, "I look forward to that." They shook hands and Robert and friends resumed their walk to shelter. Inga was very impressed with her new partner. Stephen could only laugh in amazement at what had come down moments before.

The tired group found Doug and Sandra eager to welcome their guests again. This time, Stephen brought knapsacks full of food and drink to enjoy during their visit. He also brought money, courtesy of the Black Swan Conspiracy, to aid the Morningstar alliance.

Robert was eager to know of his fellow merry explorers. "Have you heard from Charles and Isla yet?" he asked.

"They are on their way and should be here before week's end," said Richard. Our contacts say they are well."

Sandra interjected, "Come sit, and let's try some of that red wine Stephen has brought to toast our reunion." Everyone thought that a fine idea.

Three days later, a knock came on the door. Robert responded, and as the door flew open, he grabbed Isla by the waist and would not let her go. The others were warmly greeted by Doug and family. Robert was not prepared to share Isla for many moments to come.

"Oh, Isla, I have missed you and I have so much to tell," said Robert.

"I hope so," smiled Inga.

"And who might this be, Robert?" said Isla, smiling from ear to ear. Inga was waiting for an answer.

Robert blushed a little and said, "This is Inga. I found her along the way and just could not leave her behind."

"You will pay for that introduction, my love," laughed Inga. "I have heard so much about you, Isla. I am so happy to meet you."

"I have many stories I can tell of your newfound love," said Isla.

"I so look forward to hearing them," said Inga. "I am sure we will become fast friends."

"We already are, Inga," said Isla.

As everyone moved in, time was spent catching up. Isla introduced Robert to her new companions. Gab was staying until Charles and Angela arrived. Starhawk was well-known by reputation to all but Robert. Robert had met Suzanne in the spring but soon realized that Isla and Suzanne had become more than friends on the road to Morningstar. There would be a time for that story to be told. The house was getting crowded with two sets of travellers, and arrangements were made to provide sleeping accommodation nearby.

Several days later, two tired but happy people arrived at Douglas and Sandra's doorstep. It was late August, and everyone had returned. Charles and Angela eagerly revealed their marriage in Cathedral forest. Formal celebrations were to come but would have to wait for now. After new acquaintances were made and old friendships refreshed, the time had come to plan for the future.

Plans: I Won't Back Down

Doug and Sandra were busy as people came and went in preparation for a meeting called at the community hall. Word was spread and arrangements made.

As the port of Eventide was first a company town, there was no organizational structure for leadership or direction, except for the 'interests' of the companies making a profit. However, there was a network of dedicated citizens who had plans of their own for the future of Eventide, surrounding settlements, and the island.

The hall was filling quickly, and everyone found their places. Richard surveyed the crowd. The largest group were the free folk and Barney's people from Killaloo. Earlier, he had spoken with William, the New Van activist, and the few representatives from the New Life Community.

He smiled when Stephen and his Black Swan conspirators entered the front door. They joined the Eventide folks. Some faces, he didn't recognize. He expected a few came from New Harmony. Up front, were seated Starhawk, from Morningstar, and their new friends from Earthborn.

The meeting came to order and Starhawk took the floor. She began with a simple welcome and a thank you to all who were there. She talked of building an island coalition based on mutual respect for one another and their precious island home. Environmental sustainability, fair distribution of wealth, celebration of diversity, and 'do no harm' were watchwords of her speech.

When Starhawk took her seat, Richard introduced Charles and his friends from Earthborn. For the next thirty minutes, Charles described the home from where he came. The place he revealed sounded much like Starhawk's aspirations. For many, a place where power and wealth were defined by mutual prosperity was very hard to fathom.

"It works," Charles concluded. "We have found ways to prosper and grow so that everyone benefits. Our model for life is one small example of how dreams can be moulded into realities. My travels in your 'worlds' have revealed the progress you have made, although different from our own. I fear for the threat that now faces us all, but I believe we have valid alternatives to the directions that some would impose on us. I believe we can realize our dreams. We have proof that our dreams will work."

When Charles, Isla and Robert had answered many questions, the room finally became silent. From the back came a voice from someone new. A young man rose and said, "I have come from New Van. I hope I am welcome. I belonged to the district 7 militia, but no longer. I was in the East and I cannot forget what we did. I want to help."

Starhawk rose and welcomed him without reservation.

Much was discussed that night and hope was in the air. The spring could bring confrontation, and there were many who were ready to meet the challenge. The winter would be a time for preparation. Starhawk and representatives from all parts of the island would meet and prepare a list of conditions which would have to be agreed upon and met before the loggers returned.

The next day, back at Doug and Sandra's, the merry explorers and friends gathered again to reveal travelling plans before the rainy season took hold. Stephen and Michael, the ex militiaman, went to the ferry early the next morning. They would attend the scheduled meeting of the conspiracy the following week. With meetings planned, Starhawk would stay and follow later.

Gab was staying another day, and then departing on his rounds to inform others of the new developments. He asked Suzanne if she would be joining him on the trip north, but it was decided she would accompany Isla, Robert, and Inga to Earthborn. The developments in New Harmony were of concern, and Earthborn had to be seen. Of course, the most important reason was Isla.

Charles and Angela, who were now inseparable, were expected to return to Earthborn with the others. However, that was not to be for the present.

"We have a promise to keep before we join you again," said Charles. "Gab, we will join you for a time on the journey north, if we may?"

Angela added, "We have a windmill to visit. We have family there and we promised them that we would return before winter."

In Eventide, Douglas, Sandra, and Richard would work with the free folk and the villagers of Eventide. The militia were showing their muscle, and the loggers would arrive by May. How these challenges would be met required much planning in the coming months.

New Van: Brothers in Arms

The Black Swan coffee house was filled. For a conspiracy, everyone seemed very friendly and cheerful. As was expected, there were rocky roads ahead. Stephen updated the room on the Eventide meeting. It was agreed that the best defence now was a good offence. The people of New Van needed to confront the social and economic issues of their city with a unified front. The New Life Community had the organizational structures. The Black Swan conspiracy had connections in many places. Michael's input was of significance. His knowledge of the 7th District militia would be of great help as they began to plan. As the meeting broke up there was much talk of the strategy and planning to come. It was time to act.

Stephen left the Black Swan with a heavy heart. He had a stop to make. Unhappiness filled Stephen's face. He was riding the trolley to his parent's estate. The home on the edge of the city resembled a fort more than a place to live. Metal fences and rock walls surrounded the grounds. Other estates were nearby and did not look dissimilar. The controller of the waterworks for Van City lived next door. The distributor of electricity for the wealthy was farther down the way. His dad's best friend and business partner was the shipping magnate for the west coast region. These were the people who controlled New Van. These were the men who controlled the militias.

On arrival, Stephen was met by security, who escorted him to his parent's door. His mother welcomed him with open arms. His father remained in his study. After a short visit with his mother, he went to see his dad.

In the large room with little else but a desk and two chairs, Stephen sat down. His father was a good man—Stephen had always thought that—but his actions of late put much in question.

"Hello son," his father said. The coolness was evident. "It has been some time since you have been home. Is there a reason for this visit?"

Small talk didn't work with his father, so he just began, "I have been to Eventide this past two weeks," said Stephen. "There is much concern there about the behaviour of the militia. They are heavy handed and have no respect for the local citizens. There is even more concern for the loss of neighbouring forests. People live there and their homes and livelihoods are at risk, especially north of the port town. They are afraid and angry."

"We have provided jobs for many of who you speak. We created that town," said his father.

"Temporary jobs, at best, when the forests are gone," said Stephen. "The people who live in your town would now like to see it prosper," said Stephen. "I have spoken to many with good ideas for the future, Dad. I ask you to listen to them. Hear what they have to say." Stephen was then silent.

His father was visibly angry. "We have all this," he gestured an inclusive wave, "because I built it. I worked hard to gain what is ours. You have never wanted for anything and you have the nerve to question my actions." The silence was deafening.

Stephen began again, "Dad, have you seen the problems that exist for so many people here in New Van? We can do better. If we don't try, I am afraid there will be chaos in the streets."

"Life is hard, son. Some do well. Others do not. It is not my concern. I look after my own," his father answered.

Stephen rose from his chair and walked to the door. "I love you Dad. All I ask is that you listen to what they have to say." He left. His father mulled over what was said.

In the New Life community, Father Raymond and Barbara met with many civic activists. Plans were being made to stockpile food and blankets for the protests in the Spring. There were those who had done well in New Van and also wished to share their good fortune. Their resources were invaluable. Raymond had the knack for keeping people's spirits up. Around him, hope was inspired. Life was hard sometimes, but there were moments of joy and promise as well, especially when there was a mission.

Michael returned to his family and friends. They comprised of tradesmen, militiamen, working families and the unemployed, trying to survive in the city. He told them of his travels to Eventide and his connections with the Black Swan. He also had a copy of the book. When he spoke of Robert and his village, his face shone. He could imagine a better future. Some were eager to learn more. Some would rather not know. His home was a good one. His two children adored him, and he and his wife had weathered hard times with love and caring for one another. Michael felt no hatred or wrath for others but demons from the past still found him in his dreams. He hoped for peace and a good life for his children. Hope was rekindled.

Windmill Valley: You Aint Going Nowhere

On a brisk September morning, Gab, Charles, and Angela stopped at a crossroads on the trail. They rested the horses, replenished their canteens in a stream nearby, and shared a little bread and wine. Few travellers were on the roads this late in the season. Most were preparing at their homes for the winter.

"All too soon, the time has come to part ways," Gab said. "I will miss you both. You have chosen well, Angela. Charles is a good man and I expect great things for your future."

"Gab, we have been best friends for so long," Angela smiled, "Give our love to Quiet Sue, and safe journeys." Shortly thereafter, they parted. Gab veered east while his friends headed north to the Kanaar homestead.

Two days later, Charles burst out, "I can see the windmill, just beyond the pond." He took Angela's hand and they ran towards the small lean-to where they first met John. Across the pond, a tall man waved, and Rita appeared at the door to their home. Gertrude the goat was munching grass in the meadow. The horses knew the way and followed. Racing to meet them was Shanda, the border collie.

Rita met them by the pond. After hugs and more hugs, she looked at them both, "You promised to return before winter and here you are. We knew deep down you would."

Angela spoke first, "It was never in question. You both have touched our hearts in ways I did not know before we met."

John gave her another hug and slapped Charles on the shoulder. "You and I, my friend, have trails to walk and great wisdom to impart." He laughed and added. "I have missed you, my son."

As they walked to the windmill, Charles eyed the big firs not far from the pond. A grove of hemlock rose high, not far from the meadow. The big maples found in these woods were few and majestic in their presence.

Rita held the door and John was last to enter. Angela could smell the coffee. She took it upon herself to pour a cup and take it to John. Rita sat by the fire in her rocking chair and surveyed her 'family,' and was content.

In the days to come, Charles and John took many walks. Charles needn't catch John up on developments. John was kept well informed by members of his community. He and Barney from Killaloo were very good friends and met periodically. The free folk alliance was not so much an organization as a dream held by many individuals hidden away in the woods. A few often dropped into the windmill for coffee. John had known Starhawk many years ago when he lived in the city, when he and Rita had found one another and made plans.

Charles had never heard John speak ill of another human being. For John, life was to be experienced one day at a time. He was not there to judge, but to learn. However, he implied, there were people who did not have much wisdom to impart.

Angela and Rita spent a lot of time just talking. Whether it be in the garden weeding or gathering veggies for the next meal, there was always time to talk. Angela was becoming a very good knitter and developed a deep appreciation for the two sheep that bleated in the yard. Angela soon learned that Rita was the homemaker. John was the builder. He had so many skills and those he lacked, he learned from the settlers around him.

When the time was right—a phrase which seemed useful more and more often—Angela caught Rita resting in the rocker by the fire. She hesitated and then said, "Rita, I have no family that I know of. I have been on my own most of my life. When I met you and John, I felt a bond I was afraid to admit was real." She stopped.

"Let me start again," she said. "Charles and I have truly found each other. Our time in the great forest was a time of promises and commitment to each other." She continued, "I still find it hard to believe and fear the loss of it."

Rita stopped knitting and became very serious. "My dear Angela, you will not lose Charles. He comes from a place where commitment to others is at the pinnacle of his world. He has lived in a place where one could trust his feelings. His soul has not been damaged as yours has. I believe it is time for the two of you to speak your vows not only to one another, but to others, as well," Rita explained. "You need a family, my Angela. You really need a mother." She held Angela's hands. "I have some news for you that comes when 'the time is right:' I am in need of a daughter, and you would be my first and only choice." With that Angela began to cry, a cry she had been waiting for all of her life.

At that moment Charles burst through the door. "Angela, John and I have been talking."

Angela tried to laugh between tears. Charles noticed, "Is something wrong?"

"Not a thing," laughed Angela.

Charles began again, "We are going to build a house. John and I have found the perfect spot by a little stream and surrounded by an aspen grove.

John interjected, "Slowly, my son."

"John has all the plans and I will help him. It will be the shape of an A and face the stream. The deck will be magnificent." Charles was visibly excited. "We'll build a boat."

Then it dawned on him that perhaps he should get some input from Angela. "Well, what do you think?"

"I think that is the most wonderful idea," and Angela looked over to the rocking chair. "What do you think, Mom?" she asked.

It was decided they would stay the winter. Charles still had no idea what his role was to be in the developments around him. Angela didn't care for the moment.

John understood Charles' musings. "Relax, it's okay just to be," he said. Charles smiled. The first rains of late autumn had begun.

New Jerusalem: Rescue Me

Abraham's flock was already cold, and food stores were limited. Abraham promised them that God would provide. His followers on the mainland, however had not responded to their needs. Fortunately, none of the young women were with child. Celibacy was one of the sacred vows.

Jana could be found in a pew at the front of the church. She spoke to her god, "I fear we will not survive this winter, God. We need your guidance and your help." No solace came. Jana had lived on the streets after her father had disappeared. Her mother had died earlier from childbirth. She was a smart child. She lived by her wits for a period of time, however, the odds were stacked against her. If the gangs didn't claim her, the militias would.

She found help with the 'followers,' and became a sister in the flock led by Brother Abraham. But now she realized that the pilgrimage to New Jerusalem was not, in all likelihood, to end well.

As she looked up for guidance, she knew it was up to her to find shelter for herself and any others who would join her. She rose and left the church. She began to make plans and spoke with others in secret. This settlement was not a democracy. Care must be taken. Finally, several days later, she and two others packed up their few belongings and some food and fled into the night. The rowboat was there, and they floated for the big island and the unknown.

Adam, Naomi, and Jana found their way to a well-worn trail. They settled for the night and made a fire. Afraid and unfamiliar with the wild, they huddled together and hoped their god would give them a hand. They did not expect it to happen.

The next morning, they awoke to clear skies and a warmth in the air that made them smile. To her fellow travellers, Jana said, "We will find our way. There is good in this world and we deserve to find some peace."

Adam, a man who still believed in some order to his universe, could only agree. "Oh, yes, we do, and we will. The past is done. Our future will unfold as it should." He reached over and gave Naomi a hug. "It will be good. I can feel it." The sun in the sky and the warmth in the air seemed to seal the deal.

Later in the day, good fortune came their way. "Greetings, wanderers. Please join me. We will share the road for a time," a tall dark-haired young man greeted them.

Jana smiled and Adam had that look of 'I told you so.' "Well met, stranger. We are need of a friend. I am Jana and my friends are Adam and Naomi."

"You have found one," Gab responded. "What brings you here, and where might you be heading? If I may ask."

Naomi spoke up, "We don't know where we are going. And we cannot go back from where we came." The girl who spoke was younger than Jana, and still had an innocence that life had not taken away. "Will you help us?"

"Of course I will," he said. "My name is Gab and I can take you to just where you need to go."

He led the three of them down the trail. That night they slept in an empty cabin Gab knew well. The next day they arrived in a little village with a stream and a mill and several cottages.

"Welcome to Killaloo. There will be a home here if you choose to make one. There are many here who will help you if you are ready to help yourselves."

A tall older man with a long beard came to meet them. "Welcome. Call me Barney. We will make you feel at home."

Jana took Gab's hand and said, "You have shown me there is good in this world. We will make a home here and when we do, you will always be welcome. Thank you."

Gab asked from where they came. He would make a stop there and ascertain what help was needed or wanted. Her information was not unexpected.

Earthborn: A Homecoming

On the journey home, Isla was dreaming of her reunion with her family: her parents, her friends, her community. At the edge of the great forest that surrounded her little home, she noticed a large sign. It was very old and had long since been left to return to the forest. Isla dismounted and walked over to investigate further. Suzanne joined her. Robert and Inga took advantage of the pause and took some food and drink from their pack.

Isla knelt down and uncovered the old relic. It was almost unreadable. It read 'D NO EN ER, NUC EAR D MP ITE, R IATION, AN ER Suzanne knew immediately what she had found.

Suzanne read the sign, "Do not enter, Nuclear Dump Site, Radiation, Danger. There were signs like this on all sides of your village. They discouraged entry." The secret was finally out. "After the Fall, there was little left. People feared the nuclear plants that provided power. There were few left who knew how to maintain what had been built. There was no plant here, but the signs provided all the information needed to keep your secret."

Isla finally understood. How a place like Earthborn could be kept secret had always been a mystery to her. After her summer, she was glad the secret had been revealed. Isla stood and said, "Another night and we will be home."

First in sight were the windmills gently spinning in the wind. Beyond were the homes built over many years to house the few hundred souls who called Earthborn home. Well-groomed gardens and fields, freshly plowed after harvest, were a welcome sight. The orchards beyond the village were full with apples and pears. At the edge of the small lake, fed by a fast-flowing stream, was the mill.

Some things were different. As they rode, they passed many shops and buildings where villagers practised their trades. Soon, people appeared to greet them. Isla's parents were the first to welcome their daughter home, although, by all accounts, in spirit, Isla was a daughter to many. Suzanne was introduced and welcomed wholeheartedly by all.

Robert was soon found by his kin and, of course, Mary and Star, his young admirers. Robert walked his horse to Mary and hugged her vigorously.

Mary bubbled, "Have you brought stories to tell, Robert? We have missed you so much."

Star immediately noticed someone was missing. "Where is Charles?" he said. "Have you lost him?" He looked very forlorn.

Robert lifted Star off the ground, "Charles is visiting new friends in that big world out there," he smiled, "But I have brought someone with me who you are going to love." He took Inga's hand and brought her to stand before his young friends. "Inga, I want you to meet Star and Mary." The twins were in awe. A new face, and a very pretty one at that, stood before them.

Mary said, "You are very pretty. Where did Robert find you?"

Inga laughed and said, "Somewhere along the way, and he just could not leave me behind." She gave them each a hug and promised she had many stories to tell.

The days grew shorter and the rains began. Tom and Sam had been busy while Robert was gone. They took Robert to a clearing not far from town. On arrival, Robert saw many new structures—some almost built, and others just begun.

Earthborn had never grown much in Robert's lifetime. The balance between life and death seemed to be a natural one sometimes engineered by the consensus of the whole. This was most unusual.

"Our little village is changing, Robert. We have already had newcomers from the south. We expect more from the west, now that we have been introduced to the world," said Tom, as they surveyed the building site.

Sam was excited about it all. He added, "A few folks from the south have had tales to tell."

Robert interrupted, "I expect they come from New Harmony, Sam?"

"Yes. They describe a big city," said Sam quite amazed that Robert would know of this. "They are also afraid that trouble is coming. They want to stay in Earthborn and we have welcomed them."

"We have a lot to talk about, my friends. I can see my home is no longer immune to the world beyond our forest." Robert caught his breath, "There is so much to tell."

The harvest festival in Earthborn was a time of joy and celebration. The harvest had been bountiful in more ways than one. This year there were homecoming celebrations and two marriages to share. Two new couples were to be entered into the town records.

Isla and Suzanne were escorted to the centre of the hall. Wearing long flowing dresses and flowers in their hair they were formally presented to the community. They had rolls to sign and pledges to make, before their friends passed them into the hallowed place of all esteemed citizens of Earthborn. Their expression of love and commitment to one another was a ritual in which everyone wanted to share.

The second couple to be honoured were Robert and Inga. Everyone had expected that someday Isla would find her forever partner. Not so many ever figured young Robert would fall to cupid's arrow. When Inga was formally presented, it was not hard to see why Robert loved her. Her long dark hair and brown eyes shone with love and beauty. It was with much laughter and merriment that Robert and Inga were brought to the center of the hall. There were rolls to sign and pledges to make just as was previously witnessed. There was the expression of love and commitment to one another, as well. Everyone shared in this ceremony with joy. What was to come made it all even more special.

After the marriage kiss, a child appeared at Robert's side, and pulled his arm. She looked into his eyes and with innocence in her heart, Mary said, "Robert, when I grow up will you kiss me, too?"

Robert held her close and gave her a very big kiss on the cheek. Inga watched her with love and was happy.

Sam watched his friends and thought, "Someday that will be me."

The party went into the night, and the rains stopped, and the stars shone, and all was well with the world. For now.

A new era was dawning. Tom, his wife, Darla, and the elders who were with them agreed the future had promise, and the present was as it should be. Perhaps knowing the past was not so bad after all, so long as it wasn't repeated.

PART 4:

With a Little Help from My Friends

If you were alone in the universe with no one to talk to, no one with which to share the beauty of the stars, to laugh with, to touch, what would be the purpose of life? It is other life, it is love, which gives your life meaning. This is harmony. We must discover the joy of each other, the joy of challenge, the joy of growth.

Mitsugi Saotome (1937)

New Harmony: Alright for Now

In the sheltered harbour, dozens of boats sat idle in their slips. To the southern corner, large docks sat almost empty as the season for trade on the waters was drawing to an end. The fishing trawlers were still there. They hailed from New Van and were, as yet, but a few. Trade with New Van was growing, and the rumours of the militias were fresh in the minds of New Harmony's civic leaders.

After the viruses, the floods and the fires, the southern tip of the island was very limited in population. Those who remained were not accustomed to looking after themselves. Most were well-educated and managed government departments. Others were involved in trade and shipping. The basics of life were shipped in from elsewhere. Before the Fall it was a big world. When communications ceased and trade was gone, survival was in grave jeopardy. Those who remained were intelligent, but not so skilled in what was now needed to live. A small community banded together to form the Foundation of Revelation. Its tenets came from a spiritual dogma which recognized the search for spiritual awareness as the essence of life. Its primary belief was that our soul was the truth to be found in each of us. All beings were aware. We had but to realize it. They believed in our ability to find that truth, and in so doing find ourselves and find awareness.

So it was that what started as a spiritual quest became an organizational structure that not only helped them to survive in the beginning, but grew into a governing structure that brought them to the thriving city they were now. New Harmony was, by any standards, a progressive, growing city. With its foundations firmly planted in beliefs that recognized the inherent connection of all things, the city had grown in harmony with nature and respect for one another. The city had rebuilt its trade with others, and expanded its local expertise in many aspects of life. The universe was unfolding as it should. It was not just a saying; it was a belief.

Unfortunately, New Van did not share New harmony's view of reality. Protection was not a priority for New Harmony. Until now, it was not necessary. Consequently, talk of invasion and occupation by New Van's militias was not only unexpected, but unplanned for as well. There was no need for conflict. New Harmony was open to sharing its resources and expertise.

The mayor, Gordon Marchant, was speaking, "We now face a dilemma more troubling than any I have known in my lifetime." He paused and looked about the room. The councillors were as uneasy as was he. "The powerful barons across the water want our forests and our fish, and, it appears, control of our island. It seems they may be getting ready to take them."

"They do not recognize government, nor land boundaries. We need to decide how we will face this new threat to our future."

A councillor asked to be recognized. She said, "I and our delegation have just returned from Eventide. My friends, we are not alone. We have allies there and elsewhere. Good people who want the same as we do: peace to continue our life journeys in our own ways."

Councillor Anita Freeland had a fire in her eyes. The expectation that all would be well in time was never in question. She came from a family well-known for their political leanings and the passion for social justice. Her gentle, pretty face revealed a complicated young woman up for the challenge to come. She gave a synopsis of the meeting in Eventide and, in particular, the unusual news that a small village thrived just a three days ride east and north. She explained, "It has been almost alone in the world until now. It was an experiment to create a new kind of community in a new world after the Fall. I look very much forward to visiting this village soon. They live so close and have remained a secret for so long."

Shania, a young woman with native features, took the floor. "I also bring good news. Our neighbours to the north on Long Point have guaranteed their allegiance with our city and the protection of our island. As a fishing community, they have a fleet of boats that may become helpful to our efforts." Of native ancestry, she had grown up with an interest in learning of the ancient ways. She had an affinity for the remote edges of civilization and knew the dwellers of Long Point well. The 'wilds,' as the lesser populated realms had come to be called, were not unaware of the world around them. The 'ancient ways' were not unlike the values of New Harmony.

Mayor Gordon took the floor. He thanked the councillors and referenced a letter in his hands, "We have received a request from our contact in New Van. Stephen and the conspiracy would like us to help them draft a preliminary plan for civilian, democratic government in New Van. It has been decided to present a plan to the people of New Van in the summer."

In a unanimous vote, it was agreed to invite a delegation from New Van to come to New Harmony in the coming weeks. Anita volunteered to gather a committee to meet with the delegation and to draft a proposal. With all in agreement, New Harmony also committed to the support of Eventide in the spring. The final motion decided that a small delegation, headed by Shania, would go north to Long Point to ask for their assistance. In the meantime, councillors would go back to their families. How New Harmony was to deal with armed aggression was, for now, unanswered.

New Harmony's social and political structure was built on trust. Although the government members meeting were representatives of the people, they were first and foremost part of large 'family' units formed from common needs and desires for human connection. How they would respond to the present threat would be discussed and ultimately decided by a consensus, which in spirit was really one big family.

New Van: Plans

In the dorm Stephen, Cedric, John, and Rachel were in discussion regarding the reply from New Harmony. Rachel Phidd was a professor of government structures at the university. One more participant was expected, and shortly thereafter, a knock came on the door. Starhawk smiled. "I am a little late. My discussion with the local militia took longer than I expected. It seems I may have broken curfew. Don't worry. All is well. He is just a little misdirected. Nothing that can't be fixed."

Stephen welcomed her to their group, served her some coffee and introduced her to everyone. Dr. Phidd, Rachel, began, "Thank you for inviting me. My colleagues are excited about this opportunity. I would be honoured to be a representative on this endeavour, and I have a new colleague who would give anything to go with us."

"Would his name perhaps be William?" asked Starhawk.

Rachel smiled, "It most certainly is. He has spoken of you often in very glowing terms."

"I will say that I am rather impressed with him as well," said Starhawk. "He has been one of our most eager social activists in our efforts to bring together the people of this city. Father Raymond has been keeping him busy at New Life.

Cedric interjected, "I think this would be a good time to talk about how this committee should look. I believe we need a member or members who have experience in how government works, and a member familiar with the streets of New Van, rich and poor, would be of value."

John stepped in, "We need to invite someone who has not shared in the better life of this city, as well. Everyone must feel they have been represented."

The room agreed. Stephen then asked, "Do you have someone in mind, John?"

"I think so. His name is Michael. He has a small family and is currently struggling. He has a good heart and could offer much if encouraged," said John.

Starhawk then spoke, "We have done our investigations and our soul searching and we find ourselves together tonight. Let us take the next step. I believe Rachel should be on the team. William would fill the need for an activist who knows the city. I strongly agree with John's recommendation. I have met Michael and he would be an excellent addition."

"You should lead this team, Starhawk," said Stephen.

Starhawk shook her head, "Oh no, young Stephen. We all knew who would lead us even before we arrived. I recommend that the committee of four include Dr. Rachel Phidd, her colleague, William, and Michael. Stephen Cunniff will be our team's leader."

"Besides, I have work to do with our proposal from Eventide. I have some 'Barons' to meet."

"I concur," said Cedric.

"I, as well," said John. "With unanimous agreement, let us toast our new delegation."

Before the group broke for the evening, Rachel was designated to invite William. Starhawk would recruit Michael. Stephen would make preparations for their mission to New Harmony within the coming weeks. The team would be very busy informing the interested groups they would represent on their mission to New Harmony.

Killaloo: King of the Road

After Jana, Adam, and Naomi were settled, Gab spent time with Barney and Cathy. They looked forward to their times together. Late autumn was a quieter time, but Barney noted how more strangers were appearing in the area as concerns mounted in Eventide. The Alliance was prepared, but could not sustain a constant influx of new settlers. Killaloo was small and full of independent spirits.

Gab then asked about the 'mission' his three lost souls had just left behind.

"The New Jerusalem people have been known to us for some time. Brother Abraham is a strict leader, but fair, and he does have a following in New Van. This new mission, as he calls it, has caused worry. They are city people and not skilled or prepared to build from scratch. Unfortunately, we have not been encouraged to 'interfere,'" said Barney.

"Well, I think the time has come to drop in," said Gab. "Will you prepare some provisions for a group of about two dozen? I will leave day after tomorrow."

Cathy affirmed that the supplies would be ready. "You should not go alone, my friend. I have someone in mind to go with you." Gab was most comfortable travelling alone, but knew better than to argue with Cathy.

The next day, Gab made his rounds. He stopped by the dome to see their resident medicine woman. Linda was a doctor trained on the mainland. She preferred the term 'medicine woman,' as it was quite mysterious. In fact, she was well versed in medicinal herbs available in the wild. Sharing herbal tea and a rather fine blend of weed, Gab and Linda shared their stories and thanked the natural gods for their friendship.

At noon, he arrived at the mill, and was greeted by a rather portly man covered in flour.

"Aah, just in time for lunch, fair traveller. We have been expecting you. Martha has just gone for berries. Very good this time of year," laughed Josh. "The boys are in school but will want to see you." He went to the large oven and pulled out a fresh loaf of dark wheat bread. "The flour was just freshly milled from this year's harvest."

They had just sat down when Martha entered with fresh blackberries in her bag. When she saw Gab, she dropped the berries and gave him a big hug. "Welcome, welcome," she said. "We have missed you so. The boys will want to hear your newest song. You did bring your ukulele?"

"Of course, I did," said Gab. "You are my biggest fans."

They laughed and sang and when the boys arrived home from school they continued together. The boys loved their 'Uncle Gab' and he loved them too.

In the twilight, Gab came to a small cabin nestled in the hill. A candle was in the window and the fire could be seen as well. He walked up the steps and patted the old dog who sat on the mat at the door. Gab opened the door and was met by an older woman who hugged him close.

"Hi, Mom. It is so good to see you. You look well. How is Dad?" asked Gab.

"He is fine...probably asleep in his chair. He has missed you. You have neglected your chores," she laughed.

Gab entered the living room and wakened his father. After a fine meal cooked by Mom, they all sat and talked the evening away. Gab tried to be home several times a year, and sometimes for weeks at a time. He could see by the repair of the cabin and grounds that he should stay longer next trip.

Bright and early he packed and met Barney at the general store. The donkeys were loaded and his horse ready. From out of the store came Adam and Jana. They both looked refreshed and had smiles on their faces. Jana held Gab's hand and thanked him again for all he had done.

Adam simply said, "I would like to go with you Gab. They were my people and I know they need some help."

Gab smiled and shook his hand. "I will be glad for the company, Adam." Jana hugged them both and looked forward to their return.

New Jerusalem: Stand by Me

It was a cold fall day; the sky was overcast. Gab and Adam found a rowboat on the shoreline. They found shelter for the horses and loaded some supplies into the boat. Not far was the settlement of New Jerusalem. On their approach to the opposite shore, Adam could see a few familiar faces watching them. Brother Abraham was waiting as they moored the boat.

Adam greeted his former leader, and introduced Gab as his friend from a village nearby.

Brother Abraham, in a manner less than warm, said, "I recognize the wanderer. May I ask why you are here so late in the season?"

Gab stepped up and did not try to force comradery, "We help our neighbours when they have need. We have food and warm blankets. If you have further need, I know others who will help."

One of Adam's old friends came forth and embraced him. "You are an answer from God." he cried. "We are running out of good food and some in our mission are not well."

Brother Abraham pushed him aside and said, "God will provide. Sometimes we are tested."

Gab then answered firmly, "Brother Abraham, it is time to abandon this mission. The rainy season is long, and you know you are not ready to weather it." Adam had already begun to distribute the food and blankets. "There are enough provisions to get your people to Eventide. I understand you have followers in New Van who may help."

Abraham saw his followers gather to thank Adam and his friend for their assistance. They were ready to leave, and he knew he had failed to protect his flock. Abraham turned and his embarrassment was obvious. Adam came to his side.

He simply said, "We are here to help. Let us."

Abraham looked at Gab for the first time and said, "My people will prepare to leave. I believe God has sent you." A thank you was a step too far for this proud man.

This was not the first time Gab had seen faces, in despair, find hope. He had made it his life mission to provide when he could. He and Adam would get this group of good people, who were lost, to shelter with friends. He watched Adam reassure the sick and organize the able. He listened to him assure his old friends that God loved them, and they would find peace and security some day.

As they made their way across the island over the next few days, Gab thought to himself, 'I believe I may have found a fellow wanderer.' Adam smiled when he passed by Gab. He had found his purpose.

New Harmony: Feeling Alright

Stephen had known of New Harmony for many years. His father's business traded with them. His father's partner in many endeavours controlled much of the sea trade. What he did not know was how progressive and ordered this city had become.

The team of four were met by Anita and Gordon on arrival. They were trolleyed, all powered by electricity, to their quarters in city centre. Houses and apartment complexes were small and well-maintained. From what Stephen could see, there were no homeless people living in broken down buildings. The shops were busy. On first glance, the citizens of New Harmony seemed happy and prosperous.

The government buildings were beautiful ornate structures facing the marina and city docks. The city flag flew emblazed with a red carnation. Anita pointed out a sailing vessel with the name 'Force of Nature'.

"We will sail her before you return home. She is my pride and joy," said Anita. Stephen had to smile. From what he had experienced already, he was sure the sailboat was well-named.

Rachel was all business. She was peppering Gordon with questions from the time they first met. William was awestruck by the organization of this place so evident by the unquestionable feel of good governance.

Anita's friend and a city councillor walked with Michael. "Please call me Amanda," she said. "The title of councillor means little to me or any of the others. I am so glad you came, and I know we will do good work. We have done some preliminary study of New Van and have some proposals to show you."

Michael was amazed. He answered hesitantly, "This is all new to me. I have little education and even less knowledge of how government should work. I am still not sure why I am here at all."

"I have met your colleagues and I believe they have chosen you for very good reason. We are all equals here with different skills to offer," Amanda said. "I do not know what yours are, but they will reveal themselves."

Michael held his head a little higher and said with less hesitation this time, "I will take your words to heart, Amanda." Shortly thereafter, they reached the building they would call home for the next few weeks.

Every day the drafters of a new covenant for New van debated and researched not only the practical aspects of local government, but the philosophical, moral and spiritual texts from before and after the Fall. The preamble to a system of government was as important as the day to day mechanics.

Michael, who was more often a listener, spoke, "You have talked about a judicial system built on the principles of social justice and equal treatment before the law. I do not pretend to understand how to create such an entity. However, I do believe that a Bill of Rights is essential to protect those without power and influence."

Rachel answered, "Michael is absolutely correct. Although no guarantee to equal treatment, a Bill of Rights at the very least establishes the goals and aspirations.

Amanda continued, "I have examined many texts. One that stands out are the writings of Starhawk. Anita can point us to others. A Bill of Rights we will have.

Rachel added, "And Responsibilities. The two go hand in hand."

Under the supervision of Rachel, the others carefully drafted the documents. She was a legal expert in language. The others had more expertise in what they wanted to say between the words. Three weeks after the initial meeting, the draft for a new framework for New Van was ready. Everyone agreed it was far from perfect, but it was a good start. It was formally signed and printed.

Safely aboard 'Force of Nature,' Anita taught Stephen how to raise the sails. From the harbour of New Harmony, they sailed into the larger bay. Stephen was required to handle the ropes. They had another name, but he couldn't remember what it was. When Anita cried tack, he pulled and wrapped the ropes or the other way around. It was beyond Stephen why every common thing on a sailboat had to have a different name. It was also unfathomable—a nautical term—how much effort and concentration were required just to keep them afloat and moving in the desired direction.

Without doubt, this was a marvellous experience on the waves, in the wind and breathing the salt air. If Stephen hadn't been so occupied, he would have noticed Anita's soft brown hair flowing in the wind and her beautiful form as she handled her vessel. He would also have seen in his mate a vision of confidence and beauty in motion.

But that could wait. After an hour or so on the sea he implored Anita, "Might we stop and perhaps share some wine and cheese?"

Anita, busy at the wheel, looked rather puzzled. She said over the wind, "How would you propose we do that?"

Stephen quickly answered, "I have no idea. It's your boat."

Anita set the sails so that a minimal amount of concentration was required, and they toasted their good fortune between steering and handling the ropes. Back in port, with sails lowered and everything stowed, they sat on deck chairs and enjoyed the beauty of the harbour. An observer of the scene would have noted that Stephen had found some other beauty to enjoy. And she approved of his attention to such detail.

Mayor Gordon had insisted that his councillors should be given the opportunity to critique the documents. Much of the plan resembled New Harmony's government structure. However, the nature of New Van and its development to date were significantly different. In open session, the plans to create a democratically elected city council with responsibility to the people they governed was reread, and revisions put forth.

Mayor Gordon then said, "I highly recommend that the people and companies currently holding power in New Van be approached before going to the citizens themselves." It was not lost on those assembled that these were the same people and companies who may soon threaten New Harmony's peace and stability.

What began as a feeling of a job well done quickly turned into a brick wall which looked almost impossible to climb.

Anita took the floor, "We, the people of New Harmony, invited our neighbours here because they needed assistance. We did not hesitate then nor do we now. The success or failure of this brave endeavour by these four ambassadors will affect our future as well."

Stephen then stood, "We appreciate your assistance and your support for our cause. I also agree wholeheartedly that this framework must first be given to those in New Van who currently hold power." William and Michael were uneasy with such a proposition.

Stephen continued, "I have not hidden the fact that my father owns the largest logging operation on our coast. He is a major power and a threat to New Harmony and to Eventide."

"I will take our plans for the future of New Van to my father and his colleagues. I do not expect it to go well but it may not be in vain. How ever this unfolds, we must go forward. Our cause is worthy. In the past few months, I have learned one indisputable fact. We do have friends. More than I ever dreamed," Stephen said with all his heart.

Stephen and Anita spent time together over the few days left before the team went home. As well as could be, the future was planned. They agreed to enjoy the present in each other's company. Time on the sailboat was well spent. Anita sailed them to a quiet cove where a craft could be moored for the night. The evening was cool, but the cabin was full of pillows and blankets and two very warm bodies that did not seem to notice the autumn chill in the air.

Through sleepy eyes, Anita viewed her lover's face. Stephen snuggled close and slowly slipped the nightgown from her shoulder. She slipped out of her gown and revealed her body to him. Her hands unbuttoned his shirt and moved to the buckle on his belt. With Stephen's help his shirt and trousers soon dropped to the floor. Their eyes met and their bodies came together on the cool autumn evening. He kissed her. There was nothing but warmth in the cabin's bed. The night passed with soft sounds of love and passion in the air. No plans were made that night, but Stephen vowed he would learn to sail, and he had found just the teacher.

New Life Community: Plans

When William arrived at the basement of New Life Community, he was welcomed by Raymond, Barbara and several other volunteers. The place was a beehive of activity. Posters had been made and were ready for delivery to the streets. June 1st was the day set for the march through the streets of New Van. Historically, it had been a day of celebration by the 'people' in another time. It was now a rallying cry for a new day in a new city. Raymond, with a great deal of help from his partner Barbara, was organizing the rally in the park scheduled immediately following the march. Social discontent had been bubbling under the surface for many years. Raymond often asked himself why it had to be this way.

In fairness to the new barons, they had come forward in a time when chaos, famine, and violence ruled the streets. A few strong individuals had organized others to suppress the violence and to feed and house the survivors. The militias of New Van began as keepers of the peace after the Fall. Over time, the few who had restored order became comfortable in their positions of power. The peacekeepers became the private militias of the powerful. Economies grew, and gradually some of the old knowledge was rediscovered and developed. It was these few who restored the electrical grid and the water systems. Coal was rekindled as a source of heat. The trades were re-established. The fisheries were partially restored, and the forests had been given time to grow and flourish.

On the face of it, times were getting better. However, greed renewed the attack on nature, and those with power chose to keep it. The accumulation of wealth was again a driving force. Today's rulers had not learned the lessons of the past. The few, again, wanted it all.

At heart, Raymond was an optimist, but he still mused about how times had become what they were. He wondered why it had to be such a struggle to attain basic human rights. Why couldn't human beings find their way to treating all with dignity and respect? So many things were wrong.

Raymond smiled to himself, 'and we will try to set them right.' Representatives of more than thirty rights and community support groups were scheduled to speak. Social activists were excited. There was hope in the air. Change seemed to be on the horizon. 'Whatever transpires,' he thought, 'we are planning a celebration of the future, not a lamentation for the past.'

William interrupted Raymond's musings, "I have so much to tell you. The plans for our city to have a democratically elected government are ready. We would like you to present our proposal at the rally. William gave Raymond a copy and waited for his reply.

Raymond mused, "Change is in the air, and it appears I will be at the centre of it."

New Van: Father and Son

Stephen went straight to the dorm on his arrival home. Without delay, Stephen dropped a copy of 'The Framework for Local Government' on the table.

He was so glad to see his fellow 'conspirators.' "I have so much to tell you," he said. "I am excited, but I am also very fearful for what is to come. I have been to a city where so much progress has been made, and yet they are afraid for the same reasons as are we. My father and others will not like what we have to say. The values enshrined in this document are not held by them."

Cedric grabbed him by the shoulders and looked him in the eyes. He said with deep conviction, "We have built our lives on the 'values' of which you speak. You could no more walk away from them than stop breathing. We are but a few of many who are ready to live by our beliefs."

John then chimed in to lighten the air, "And besides, we're the good guys, and the good guys always win."

Stephen sat in the only chair left vacant, and his expression demanded attention. "I have some other news and it is very good. I have met someone, and I think she may be the one. Her name is Anita. The room was silent. Stephen was not one they expected to reveal such news so readily. They all smiled.

Cedric ended the silence and couldn't resist asking, "And what does she think of you?"

John added, "She is probably a figment of his imagination. It was a long trip."

"I'll have you know she thinks I am very smart and have an excellent body," laughed Stephen.

"It is quite obvious that New Harmony has a serious lack of eligible bachelors," said John.

Stephen gave up and succumbed to the teasing. He was happy to be home, but he did miss that girl. The evening was good for Stephen. Sometimes you just need a little help from your friends. Tomorrow he would see his father and he would need all the help he could get.

In his study, James Cunniff and his son sat opposite one another in the only two chairs in the room. The 'Framework for Local Government' sat on the desk. Conversation was erratic. Communication between father and son had never been easy for them.

Stephen began, "Dad, I know we have had our differences and you have always tried to be fair. I cannot explain to you as well as I would like how I view my world. I have been to New Harmony and seen what a city that works for all the people can be like. There are good people in New Van who at present have very difficult lives. We can build a great city here if we all work together. Please read this. We would like your input and ultimately your support."

His Dad, James, stood and walked to the window. The room was silent. He finally answered, "You have been busy, my son. I always suspected that you would become a leader. In fact, I planned for it," his father said. "However, your initiative now is not what I envisioned." He clasped his hands.

"I grew up in a different place than the one you live in now. I do not believe that what you want is possible yet, if ever. I will not give up my power or my position and my colleagues are probably more rigid than I. However, I will bend enough to read your proposal and to either reject it fully or suggest changes I can accept. I will convene a meeting of my peers to consider your 'framework.' Mark my words: I do not expect much, as we have not survived by negotiation and compromise. You are asking for a great deal from us."

Stephen looked at his father with a new appreciation for who he was.

James Cunniff concluded with one demand. He addressed his son, "I will do as I have said, son, but you must promise to inform me of all developments on your side as this conflict unfolds. I do not know what is to come, but it may not be good. Do I have your word?"

Stephen's prior optimism faded, "I cannot give you information that might put my friends in jeopardy. I just can't."

James looked directly at Stephen with some pride, "I would never have expected you to. All I need is information to give me some understanding as to the nature of your endeavour."

Stephen shook his father's hand and said, "That I can do."

Long Point: New Faces

Shania and her small delegation from New Harmony arrived by boat at the peninsula of Long Point, several miles north of the city. Nestled in a protected harbour, a fleet of fishing boats were moored, and the village spread out beyond it. She was met by a group of confident, dark-haired native people. Although trade had been steady with this community for several years, social contact was still limited. These were a private people and Shania respected that. That afternoon, they gathered in the great hall. It was layered with animal skins, and the decor suggested this was a lodging as well as a meeting place. Tradition had been virtually destroyed after the Fall. There was little left to hang on to, but the hall suggested these people had not lost all of their heritage.

Chief Commanda, as she was called, and her elders, listened attentively to the information Shania and her people brought to them. Shania spoke of the destruction of the forests in Eventide and the challenge to come in the spring. She talked of New Harmony and the people's fear of losing all that had been built. She spoke with respect and humility and awe for the natural wonders that were shared by all peoples.

As they listened, the chief and her elders could feel Shania's concern. She was asking for guidance and aid, if there was any to be given. It was not unknown to them how their environment, their home, was once more being put at risk. The name Haida Gwaii was spoken many times in her description of her island home. The words were sacred to them, but Shania did not yet know their meaning.

Before leaving the meeting place, a ceremony was held to ask for blessings from the gods of nature. In front of the tall totem on the harbourfront, the chief honoured Shania with a traditional bow. She said, "We have heard your plea. Do not fear. There is hope in the wind and we will meet before the sun is high in the sky."

Shania and her delegation bowed and boarded their vessel. She could feel the wind, but was not sure what direction it would take.

Earthborn: Home Fires

November was a dreary month in the village of Earthborn. It was a time to enjoy the fruits of their labour. The cottages glowed with yellow-orange flames in the fireplaces. In the woods and meadows of Earthborn, residents rose with the sun and retired not long after the moon appeared.

The new homes were completed and the few who came from New Harmony were comfortably housed, as were Isla and Suzanne, who had wanted a place of their own. Robert and Inga chose to live in his parent's home. They both enjoyed the closeness of loved ones.

Suzanne had sent messages to Morningstar via the wanderer, a new one, since Angela had gone on vacation. Although she missed her mother and her library, she had found a new calling since she left home. A new age was beginning, and it needed to be chronicled. She and Isla agreed that this was a task worth pursuing.

In their new living room, one young woman sat in front of the fire. It had burned almost to coals and would soon need a log to rekindle the fire. A chess board, with a game half finished, sat idle on the table. Already a bookcase in the corner was half full and a desk nearby was covered with papers. Suzanne was reading a book. Isla entered with two cups of steaming tea. She placed the mugs on the table, went back to the kitchen, and returned with a cup of fresh cream and a jar of honey.

She sat down on the couch. Suzanne reached for the tea. "Let it steep." said Isla. Suzanne leaned back in her chair. She waited for Isla's next remarks.

"Where do we go from here?" said Isla idly. It was almost a rhetorical question. "Our road already has taken so many turns." She smiled to herself as she reflected on her recent journeys.

Suzanne sat up in the big chair a few feet away. She looked at her and smiled. 'To think, she loves me and I her.'

Suzanne closed her book. Reading obviously was not an option. "It really doesn't matter as long as we're together," she answered. That could have been a satisfactory end to the conversation, but Suzanne had an inkling Isla wanted to talk.

"I have had many conversations with our new friends from New Harmony. I believe that our neighbour to the south is becoming a major player in this bigger game of chess." Suzanne began. "We are rather unique here on the Island. Our communities seem to reflect the better angels of our world. We have a neighbour across the water, however, that was born again out of power and greed. How we resolve this great divide is to be the stuff of a new history. The testaments have been written. We are living in a new book."

Isla answered, "If we are to write this book, we have some decisions to make. Earthborn will have its role in this new book but there are chapters to be written before what Earthborn has to offer will be read or understood."

Suzanne looked again at the fire and the woven rug. She eyed the bookshelf she loved so much, and the kitten sleeping by the fire. "I knew this was too good to be true. Where do you see us going and when?"

Isla sat back in her chair. "In the spring, I think we should go to Eventide. I have a feeling we will find many pages to write. I just hope we have some happy endings to record. She grabbed her mug and sipped her tea. "Besides, we have some good friends to visit."

Seeing it was now a safe time to drink her tea, Suzanne added some honey and a small bit of cream. She took a drink and smiled at her partner, "I think that is a very good plan."

More than satisfied with Suzanne's response, Isla patted the couch beside her and said, "We have lots of time before we go, and I want to make very good use of it."

Suzanne joined her on the couch and sighed, "So much for my book and cup of tea." Much later someone put a new log on the fire.

Not far down the road, another couple had settled in for the evening. Robert's folks loved Inga, and the feelings were mutual. Mom and Dad were more than pleased to have their son and new daughter live with them. Robert's sister was ecstatic. Robert took no time to settle into his old life. He and Inga found their niche in the multitude of jobs that always needed to be done. They brought a perspective to Earthborn that was valued by its citizens. They both had a great deal to offer. Inga loved the land. Tom, the elder, valued Robert's insight, and the two became very good friends. Strategies for Earthborn's future development were often discussed. Of course, there was always time to sit with Star and Mary and their friends. He had stories to tell, and a promise was a promise. Robert was loved by the children and he loved them. Inga fit perfectly into this little world. Raven, in particular, had a very large crush on her. She had been a city girl. Inga had studied horticulture on the chance that someday she would be able to apply those skills. It now appeared she would get her chance. She would be a farmer.

Of his future, Robert often wondered. He had loved his time in Eventide and the friends he made. He even missed Boris and his pals. He wondered if he might yet see Boris again. His friends in New Van, he missed most of all. For the Black Swan Conspiracy, he had a special place in his heart. Life at university certainly had its appeal. Cedric's recitations of Shakespeare would always be remembered as magical. And Inga, beautiful, kind, loving Inga...

He had almost dozed off when Inga came into the room in her night clothes. She took his arm and whispered, "Hurry, I need you to keep the bed warm."

Robert knew at that moment, when all was considered, Earthborn was home and he belonged here. They belonged here. He was truly blessed.

Next to the marketplace, the sturdy log home sat beneath the stars. Sam lived here with his parents. Sam Bachus' ancestors had built this house and the Bachus clan had lived there ever since. Sam had never left Earthborn and, until recently, never expected he would. However, lately there was a new wrinkle in the Earthborn quilt. Everyone felt it and most just thought it would unravel in time. Sam was not one of those. He was restless. Of late he spent many hours under the old maple peppering Robert with questions about Eventide and New Van. He was fascinated when Suzanne told him of Quiet Sue and the village of Killaloo and the trails. Last thing before retiring for the night, it was Sam's pleasure to take Frodo out for his nightly run. Frodo was Sam's dog and each night he relished the short run beneath the stars. As Frodo disappeared into the woods Sam looked up at Orion.

Sam talked to the sky, "I will see the wonders of this new world." Frodo came to his side for a pet. Sam rubbed his head and said, "How would you like to go on a journey?" Frodo licked his hand and they went into the house. The stars of Orion winked as they retired for the night.

As it always did, the sun rose the next morning, although it couldn't be seen for the clouds. By noon, the sky had cleared somewhat. It was then that a new face arrived on horseback. She rode into town and knew just where she was going. At Tom's house, she dismounted, gave her horse some oats and water and went to the door. She was invited in and offered food and drink and a chance to wash the miles from her tired body. Cody introduced herself as the wanderer. In her pack were letters. She also had personal messages she was asked to deliver.

By the time the afternoon waned, Cody had spoken to Tom of Starhawk's trip to New Van and the plans being made. Robert and Inga had arrived by invitation.

Cody approached them both and gave them big hugs. "Personal greetings from John," she said in all seriousness. "You are as he describes you. He misses you both very much. And Robert you are to play your mandolin for me before I go."

Robert, so happy he could burst, said, "Perhaps we should practice my message back to John?"

Inga kicked him in the shin and said, "Perhaps not." She laughed and took Cody's hands, "Give him my best. I miss him dearly."

Darla, Tom's wife, hugged her man and gave him a big kiss too.

Cody settled in just like family, and they enjoyed each others company. Robert played the mandolin and Inga joined in with the harmonica. Tom played guitar and Darla pulled out the spoons. Everyone sang.

Sam heard the merriment from the street and hurried to join them. He was like a kid in a candy shop. There was Robert, part of the Black Swan Conspiracy, Inga, a real city girl, and now Cody, a real-life wanderer. If Isla and Suzanne appeared, he would not believe his good fortune.

On cue, the door flew open and Suzanne and Isla came, hand in hand with more food and drink. This was too much for Sam.

He surveyed the room, stood up with a tear in his eye and announced with conviction, "Next expedition I'm going. I can't stand it any longer."

Everyone cheered him on. Tom said to his young friend, "I believe it is time for you to see the world." He was almost in tears. "I can think of no better ambassador."

Darla completed the thought, "You will be in very good company on your journeys. Tom and I will miss you."

"We'll take very good care of you Sam," said Isla. "Just be careful of those local girls. They are very clingy." Suzanne concurred.

Robert caught the implication. He looked at Isla and asked, "Where are you going?" The room grew silent. Everyone listened.

"We will be going to Eventide in late March. The loggers are coming and the campaign to stop them requires all the help it can get."

Cody confirmed the information and that she had delivered messages from Eventide to Tom earlier in the day. "I bring greetings from Douglas, Sandra, and Richard as well. They all miss you very much and cannot wait to see you."

Robert and Inga both knew their plans had changed. Inga said, "If we may, we shall join you. We shall be the merry explorers once again." Robert walked over to Sam.

Sam stood frozen in his boots in anticipation. Robert patted him on the shoulder and laughed, "We expect you will be packed and ready to go when we head out? We abide no stragglers."

Sam just sat down in his chair. It was just too much for young Sam. Tom started strumming his guitar. Isla grabbed the tambourine. The others were ready to join in and continue the celebration. After all, the leaving time was months away. Robert yelled, "Tom, let's do 'Ride me High.'"

Eventide: For What Its Worth

April came in like a lion. The waters between New Van and Eventide were rough, as the winds were high. Already the herring had run the channel and the fishing had begun. The salmon fishing looked promising. To the southwest of town was the fish factory, and some workers had already returned to work. The sea lions had also returned, gorging on the rich herring schools. In Eventide, the dogwoods and the cherry trees were blooming bright pink and white, the only real colour in the streets. It was not a pretty town, Eventide's buildings were built quickly, with utility in mind, and the streets were muddy. It was a port built to access fish and lumber. To the barons of New Van, the people and the environment were peripheral to their needs.

Awareness of a wider community on the island north of Eventide was irrelevant for James Cunniff and his peers. For them, the island was a resource to be harvested. Stephen had tried to explain to his father that there were people here; villages and towns made up of people building their lives. As promised, he had also warned him that unrest was building against his father and his powerful friends. He warned his father that he could expect trouble in the spring.

Eventide was waking from the winter. Spring was here. Many houses, mostly row houses and dorms, were empty and would house the loggers later, once the logging season began. Across the bay, the ferry came just once a week at this time of year, its coal-powered engines reminiscent of another not so desirable time.

The few year-round residents lived in duplexes, and some had single log and plank homes. Over the winter, the community grew close. Survival was tenuous. Helping one another was essential to island life. For early April, the village was unusually busy.

The mill was idle until the logs started running. The whistle to start the working day was silent. The big docks were ready for the barges to transport the finished lumber. James Cunniff, the lumber baron, and Peter Scott, his shipping financier, had found new consumers for their lumber and fish in places along the coast to the south. Business was brisk and there was money to be made. To date, nothing had slowed their progress. Certainly, a few back woods free folk would not get in their way. The trees here were plentiful and easy to harvest. The salmon were running again.

In the east corner of the village, the militiamen were housed. There was a small contingent at this time. The streets were quiet, and the militiamen were getting lazy. Boris, the boss, was reading the last message from his superiors in New Van. The new system relayed messages across the water. The message boded of dark times ahead.

He read the message to himself.

> "Informed local citizens organizing to stop island logging operations.
>
> Militant group called the 'free folk' are expected.
>
> Strength is unknown.
>
> The Black Swan conspiracy terrorist group may be involved.
>
> City of New Harmony sending insurgents.
>
> More recruits coming on the Wednesday ferry.
>
> Use of lethal force is authorized if necessary."

Even in the working season, Boris' main concerns were drunken loggers. His men were adept at handling bar fights, and the fear they instilled in the local citizens made life easy for Boris and his men. What was written here was of grave concern. His spies had informed him of the meeting in September, but nothing had come of it. Besides, the barons didn't pay well enough for him to work too hard. He put the message down and went back to his barracks. He figured he best do some checking tomorrow, but it could wait until then. In his favourite chair, he drank his second ale and thought about how he got here. Good options for a man like him were not many. He was born poor and expected it wouldn't change. When he was a boy, the streets were rough. There was no real order on his side of the city. Life was day to day and often brutal. When the opportunity came to join the security force, he took it. Life in the 7th District Militia was good. When he was promoted and sent to Eventide, it started well. The longer he lived here, he realized, the more he liked the locals that he was hired to keep in check. For his new friend, Robert, he had good thoughts. Another ale and he would call it a night. It appeared his life would get more complicated this spring.

In a house on the west side of town, Sandra and Douglas were very busy welcoming their friends as the gathering began. Charles and Angela arrived earliest. They were eager to hear news of their beloved Earthborn and the adventures of their friends. Robert, Inga, Suzanne, and Isla came shortly thereafter. With them came a new face and a wire-haired terrier wagging her tail.

Sandra ushered in Sam with a warm hug and said, "Welcome to the conspiracy. You are travelling in good company, young man." She paused, "And who are you?" She reached out and patted a furry head.

"Sandra, Douglas, please meet our friend Sam, and Frodo, his faithful companion," said Robert. "Sam could not leave her behind." Inga gave Robert a dirty look.

"We are glad you have come, Sam and Frodo. Your friends have told us all about you," said the man of the house. He shook his hand. "I am Douglas. I fear you have come in sad times."

Sandra added with a smile, "But there will be some very happy times as well, and this is one of them." She took Suzanne's hand

and said, "Remember that case of red wine Stephen brought? Come with me. We need to talk."

In the living room, Douglas passed on Richard's regrets for his absence. The house was more than full, and yet everyone there, except Sam, knew there was still one face missing.

Just north of town, a small village of tents and other temporary shelters were multiplying. In one of the two more permanent buildings, a man with a beard and spirit in his eyes was busy setting up the 'Church of the Nazarene' kitchen. He and his small group of followers were going to feed the gathering of free folk. His story was a familiar one among those who were born again in her grace. He had seen the light on his journey back to Eventide, and was answering the call to serve the people.

Gab and his new protégé entered the building and approached the busy bearded man. The tall, lanky and rather formal man turned and smiled.

"Adam and Gab come, come, sit, and let us share a meal. I am so glad to see you," said the man. He was raised much too formally to embrace his acquaintances but his pleasure for their company was obvious.

Gab gave him a hug anyways. He looked almost in awe. "Well if this does not beat all. Brother Abraham, it is so good to see you. You are a different man from the one I left here a few months ago."

"Yes, I am, son, and you are partly responsible for my salvation. As are you, Adam," said Abraham in all seriousness. "I have found the light." Abraham gave the blessing, and they shared one of many meals Abraham and his flock would provide in the coming days.

In the camping grounds, Richard was busy helping the free folk and the emissaries from Killaloo get set up. Barney was there playing his fiddle and keeping everyone's spirits up. Jana, the newest resident of Killaloo, had come with him. She had skills in nursing and was helping Linda, the medicine woman, set up the treatment centre in the building next to Brother Abraham's kitchen.

"Let me get that for you," said Richard as he moved a table for the young lady he didn't know. "I'm Richard. I live here, and I am at your service."

In her shy but confident way she answered, "Thank you. I am Jana. It is very nice to meet you." Richard smiled and thought he might spend a little more time helping his new acquaintance.

In a secluded glen near the southwest docks near the fish factory, Raymond and William decided they would make camp. They had many volunteers who had arrived from New Van by private boat under cover of night. The unloading of vast quantities of rope took several hours. Large horses were being led to the new paddock. Raymond and William had their part to play, and plans were in motion. At least for now, they were hidden from the militia.

The next morning, the ferry arrived from New Van, and several more faces walked down the ramp ready to support the people of the island. Starhawk came first, followed by a clearly troubled face. Anyone could tell they carried news that no one wanted to hear. The two made their way to the house in the west end of town. Starhawk had just come from meeting with Stephen's father and others who controlled the company town of Eventide. As they approached the house, many people were waiting on the front lawn. Stephen had finally arrived, and his friends gave him the welcome he so sorely needed. The last had arrived and everyone went inside. All but Starhawk. She went to find Barney and the folk from up north.

No word had come as yet of the contingent from New Harmony. To be sure, the promise was made. No one doubted it would be kept. The people of New Harmony would come. The day was cloudy, and rain came in short intervals, but every once in awhile, the sun peeked out and seemed to imply that all was not grim and hopeless.

In the community hall two days later, people were gathering. Starhawk wasted no time. She recounted her meeting with the barons of New Van. Stephen emphasized that the men and militia who threatened their livelihood had no intention of backing down, and they would be armed. He ended with, "There has been violence elsewhere, and it can and should be expected here."

In a speech that would be remembered long after the events of the next few days, Starhawk reminded everyone of who they aspired to be and of the future they were trying to build:

"My friends, my family, our lives are built on sacred principles. We have come here to our Island to find peace and communion for our souls. We envision a world where we live in harmony with nature, where She will provide for us and we will respect and nourish her. We are Gaia.

We believe in the soul and physical connection of all things.

We believe in the sacredness of all lives.

We are finding new ways to live with
one another and to thrive. We are learning to love.

We have a sacred duty to act as we believe.

We must lead by example, not only for us but for the good of all.

We will resist. We will find ways to confuse
and deter, to stop and to persuade our aggressors.

We will not kill. We will not use weapons.
And we will overcome.

We will build our world. We will make a difference.

We are children of the universe and we have a right to be here."

Not a whisper could be heard as Starhawk took her seat. Not everyone in the hall could support what she had said. Self preservation was a powerful human trait. Yet in their hearts, they knew that peaceful resistance might be their best and only viable option. In the back row Quiet Sue said to herself, "I am ready to protect my dream."

Boris was aware of the meeting but thought it best not to intervene until he had a few more men. Many people—one hundred or more—had arrived in Eventide already, and they did not come to support him. His reinforcements were expected in two days time. He was uneasy. These were simple, hardworking folk. Many came as families. They were not fighters. But neither did they look like they would back down.

The Day of Reckoning: A Time to Act

The Wednesday in mid April began as a quiet spring day, with clouds in the sky and a glimmer of sun at times. The channel was calm, and it was clear enough to see New Van on the horizon. The whistle from the mill sounded three long, shrill notes. From the houses and the campsites, people answered the call and began to gather at the docks. Within minutes, two hundred or more people were assembled.

The ferry was still thirty minutes away, smoke from its engine visible in the channel. Boris gathered his militia at the barracks in east Eventide. He gave instructions to secure the dock. They were well armed with clubs and knives. Boris emphasized, "Use only necessary force." As his men approached the crowd, Boris watched.

The wall of people on the shore were a mix of young and older. Some were obviously dwellers of the wilder regions. Others were just villagers standing as family watching the approach of the ferry. Everyone was scared. He could see that. Most of the permanent citizens of Eventide had joined the throng. Some, Boris assumed, were hiding in their homes. A bearded older participant played his fiddle and tried to reassure his neighbours. A few sung along with him. Some tried but soon went silent.

Most of the wilder-looking free folk stood at the front of the crowd. If trouble began, they appeared to be tougher and more defiant. From the west, a new group appeared. They were not from here. They looked organized and confident. Boris was sure they must be recruits from New Van.

As Boris' militia raised their clubs to push back the crowd, there was one more thing he noticed. None of them had weapons. He came as close as was possible where he could still direct his men. There were no weapons. The closest thing to a weapon was the fiddle.

Boris said to himself, "What have I found myself in? I like a good fight, but this is not it."

First contact began as the protesters held their ground. Clubs were wielded and islanders fell, bloodied by the blows. The militiamen pressed forward, and new folk stood their ground. They, too, were knocked down. Their comrades helped take the injured back to safety. The medical unit was busy. Linda and Jana cleaned wounds and bandaged cuts. It took the militiamen quite some time before they secured the dock. Dozens of islanders were injured, but the protest remained strong. Boris could control his men. They had shown restraint. He was not so sure about the new recruits on the approaching ferry. A few hundred yards from the dock, the ferry slowed. Its decks were filled with young recruits. Boris knew they were well trained, and many would have seen battle before.

Much to Boris' surprise, the throng began to chant, "This is our home. We will protect it."

The voices grew louder, "All we are saying is give peace a chance." It was sung and chanted over and over again.

Then a loud rumble could be heard from the docks loaded with militiamen. Less than one hundred yards away, the ferry stopped. The docks began to wobble and the log pylons beneath the docks crumbled. The militiamen lost their balance, and many were thrown into the water. Without their footings, the huge docks twisted and fell into the harbour. From the shore, men with horses secured with ropes tied to the docks' pilings could be seen cheering as the docks crumbled. Boris' men were in the water. Many did not know how to swim.

What happened next would be chronicled by Isla in poetry and by Suzanne in prose. Musicians would make songs about this day. Boris watched as the chanting stopped and the protesters jumped into the water to save the drowning militia. The crowd made room for men to be brought ashore. Those who had been injured in the fall were taken to the medical building for treatment. In short order, everyone was safe on shore.

Boris, after joining the rescuers, stood on shore dripping wet. He looked out at the ferry, still stationary, a few hundred yards from the dock. Behind it, two dozen or more boats in full sail approached the harbour. As they surrounded the ferry and Eventide's cove, they lowered their sails and cheered. The flag of Eagles soaring could be seen on every boat. Beside the Eagles were the flags of New Harmony, emblazed with a red carnation.

Stephen, standing on the shore cheered, "I knew you would come."

The ferry turned around and signalled it would return to New Van. The armada gave it room and it grew smaller on the horizon. On shore, the crowd began to thin. The ships made anchor and the sailors prepared to disembark.

As if by divine intervention, the clouds disappeared, and the sun shone. The people of the island had won the day. As the natives of Long Point later explained, 'people of the island,' in their ancient language, was interpreted as Haida Gwaii.

Robert came up beside Boris and shook his hand. "You did well today, my new friend," he said. We would like you and your men to join us. There is food and drink and we will gather later in the hall."

Boris could not believe his eyes or ears. "Robert, my friend." He patted Robert's shoulder, "Yes," he said. "We will be pleased to join you."

A Time to Laugh: Turn, Turn, Turn

Bright and sunny was the afternoon. Small boats were sent out to gather the sailors from the armada. First to disembark was an impressive figure escorted by a raven-haired beauty and a brown-haired goddess. Stephen rushed to meet them. With the minimum of protocol, he greeted the Chief and embraced Anita.

Anita spoke first, "I would say our debut was almost perfect timing, you handsome man."

"It certainly was, and you sure know how to make an entrance," laughed Stephen. "I am so happy to see you." He kissed her again and would not let her go.

At this point, the dark-haired woman stepped in, "Excuse me, sir, we were told we would be welcomed with open arms when we arrived." She was smiling. "I assume your name is Stephen?"

"You are correct, and I do apologize for my shoddy welcome," said Stephen, as he put out his hand in greeting. The raven-haired beauty gave him a hug instead.

"My name is Shania," she said. "I thought you might never ask."

By this time, fortunately, Chief Commanda had been met by Richard and a host of others. Shania joined the group and introduced the chief properly to her hosts. They left the docks, and Richard led the chief and Shania to lodgings left available for just such guests. Hand in hand, Stephen and Anita walked to Doug and Sandra's.

Many of the sailors chose to stay on the boats. The few that chose to land were housed near their chief.

The Church of the Nazarene kitchen was abuzz. In the chaos of providing hot meals to the many gathered in the building, Brother Abraham was in his glory. Thankfully, he had lots of volunteers.

Even Naomi, his former follower, volunteered her help. She had come from Killaloo with Jana.

Naomi was ladling thick pea soup to hungry folk. In line was a young man with curly blondish hair, followed by a funny looking dog with a long tail. She thought she would like to meet this boy. When he reached out his bowl, she gave him a very big scoop. He looked up, and his blue eyes caught her brown ones. He stopped and was, for a moment, speechless. Finally, he said, "Hi, I'm Sam." That was the extent of it.

She just said, "Hi." Then she added, "My name is Naomi."

By this time, the line was getting longer and there were a few whispers. Sam blushed and moved along. Behind him a voice whispered in his ear, "I think she likes you."

He looked around to see a very tall blonde lady all dressed in leather. She said, "Hi Sam. The world is quite exciting, isn't it? It is nice to see you again."

Sam was awestruck. "Cody! Come sit with me. It has been quite a day." They found a table and Frodo just wagged his tail.

Linda and Jana had seen their last patient. There were no life-threatening injuries, but a few of Boris' men suffered broken limbs. They were set and would be fine in a few weeks. Hungry and tired, the doctor and nurse headed for the building next door. On their way, Richard met them.

"Allow me to escort you, ladies. You have had a very long day," said Richard. "I will find you a seat and will deliver your meals right to your table."

Richard had become Eventide's and the free folk's chief organizer. The orderly unfolding of the uprising was primarily to his credit. He was esteemed by many. So, when he cleared room at a table and went to the front of the line to collect three meals with all the trimmings, no one said a thing.

Linda thanked him very graciously. Jana gave him a kiss on the cheek. "Without a doubt, this has been a good day," he said to himself. Feeling quite daring, he finished his meal and asked Jana, "Perhaps I may have a dance later in the hall."

"That would be nice. Yes," said Jana. Linda watched the encounter unfold and was happy for her young protégé. They finished their meals and went back to their tent to prepare for the evening.

At a fire in the free folk camp, Abdul had come to see his old friend Barney. Around the fire sat Gab and Quiet Sue. Cody and Sam had just arrived after their supper, laughing and telling stories. Near the fire, Frodo curled up and slept. Barney was playing his fiddle. From out of the woods nearby came Charles and Angela.

Abdul jumped from his seat on an old log and cried, "Sparkle and Rosebud. Come here and let me look at you." He looked at Angela up and down. "You look good, Rosebud. Sparkle must be living up to his name."

"Oh, he is," laughed Angela. She looked Abdul up and down, "You look much different in clothes, my dear friend."

By this time, Barney stopped playing and came over to welcome the new guests. Barney and Abdul went off to talk and reminisce. Gab greeted Angela very warmly and appraised Charles to see if he was good enough for his very old friend.

Charles spotted Sam and sat down beside him. He gave Frodo a pat. Sam introduced him to Cody. She was more than pleased to meet the famous Charles. Killaloo weed, also famous, was being generously shared around the campfire. A joint was passed from Cody to Sam to Charles and on. Moments later, Sam began to giggle. Cody looked at Sam and started to laugh. Having no idea why, Charles was laughing as well. Nothing seemed to be funny, but that obviously didn't matter.

Out of nowhere, Sam said, "I'm hungry." Then everyone laughed.

Quiet Sue was quite content just to watch as her friends communed with one another around a warm fire.

Back at their home, Douglas and Sandra prepared dinner for Stephen, Anita, Shania, and Chief Commanda. Sandra thrived on doing for her guests. She was a true Taurus from the stars. When Shania arrived with the chief, she introduced her as Ahana. This was not a time for formality. Sandra took that as a great complement. They were among friends.

The table was alive with stories.

Ahana, meaning inner light, captured them all with her tales of the ancient traditions. She described their island as a living, breathing entity. Her emissaries were the ravens and the wolves and the salmon and the great whales in the vast ocean. Haida Gwaii was sacred.

Shania loved the wild lands and cherished her connection with the people of Long Point. She also spoke with passion of other peoples she called the "wilds." They lived in lands south of the island and north.

Of these new lands, Stephen was very interested. Anita had sometimes talked to him of these people. Someday he would meet the people of these lands.

Sandra could not believe her ears. She held her husband's hand and rubbed her head on his shoulder, "We are truly blessed to have such friends."

After Ahana had blessed the gathering, Anita stood and looked to Douglas and Sandra and said, "This has been a wonderful time together. Thank you for sharing your home and your love. We are truly blessed to have you as our friends. You are truly family."

In a cottage on the town's edge, Starhawk was meeting with Suzanne and Isla. They had not seen one another for too long. Suzanne and Starhawk talked fondly of Morningstar; they had not been home for many months, and they agreed it was time to go home. Isla concurred.

Starhawk had one more mission to complete. "We will go together when it is done," she said. "First, I must go back to New Van and settle this dispute at least for this season. I believe we have some leverage now. Perhaps they will listen."

"We will go with you," said Suzanne. She gave an inquiring look to Isla.

"Yes," said Isla.

"Thank you, but no. Richard will accompany me. He will represent our island well and be here when we leave," said Starhawk. "When I return, I look forward to our journey north."

In the pub, some of Boris' men and a few of the locals had filled the tables. At first, the atmosphere was frosty. The day had been horrific for both sides. Both the militia and the locals were concerned about their futures. A few wore slings and many had cuts and large bruises. Through the door came Boris and a man none had seen before.

"Barkeep, the best ale in the house for my new friend, and one for me, of course," bellowed Boris. "Mates, meet Michael. A former militiaman in New Van, and a very fine chap." They had met while saving his men that morning. "A toast to the fine men who rescued my mates."

Michael, a little less boisterous, responded with, "A toast, as well, to the militiamen of Eventide who performed their duties with honour and restraint."

That was enough to crack the ice, and in the course of the afternoon, animosities lessened and some new friends were made. Boris would be needing more militiamen. He wondered if Michael might consider working for him.

When Boris went back to his dwelling, he found a new message. He sat in his favourite chair and hoped this was going to be good news. He read:

Received today's news.

Received your assessment.

Contact Starhawk and Eventide leader.

Will meet in New Van offices one week from today.

Confirm message and respond.

James Cunniff

"All may yet be well," he thought.

A Time to Sing and a Time to Dance

It was still quite early when the community hall started to fill. The frame building built from local timber and milled in Eventide, was a favourite meeting spot. Tonight, they would dance.

On stage, Barney and Abdul were setting up their chairs. Standing was for younger folk, they both agreed. The fiddle and Abdul's ukulele were in their stands.

When Inga and Robert arrived, Inga pushed him to the stage. She said, "Your mandolin is already there, and Abdul knows you are joining them."

Quiet Sue came on stage and sat behind two drums already set up for her.

At one of the few tables sat William, the Van City activist, with Stephen and the rest of his entourage. It appeared he was re-enacting the pulling down of the docks with ropes and horses. His audience was losing interest. After all, they had been there.

Richard came to the stage and welcomed everyone. He then introduced the band. By this time, Anita, Isla and Suzanne had joined the crew. They were introduced as the back-up singing trio. There still seemed to be one essential piece missing. Robert spoke to Abdul.

"Patience, my boy. We are not all here yet." said Abdul.

With a guitar in hand and a smile on his face, John from New Van appeared from the already full hall. Robert ran to his dear friend and fellow musician and ushered him onto the stage.

Without further delay, the band played. There were folk tunes Barney had learned in his time in Killaloo. They were made for the fiddle. With his ukulele, Abdul played some silly songs like 'Tiptoe Through the Tulips' in falsetto. With back-up from Robert, John took centre stage and played 'Shelter from the

Storm.' The audience was ecstatic. John was quick to credit the trio for their excellent vocals.

On the dance floor, couples held one another in one of the slow dances of the night. Sam finally asked Naomi to dance. Adam—the newest member of the wanderers and Gab's protégé—was dancing with his colleague Cody. Sandra was most interested in the couple not far from their table: her dear friend Richard was dancing with the new nurse from Killaloo. He looked happy.

After a short break, the band reassembled and introduced John again with his new song. It had been a memorable day and a remarkable year. John dedicated his song to all those friends and 'family' who came together for one another and a cause worth fighting for. It was called 'With a Little Help from My Friends.'

You Can't Always Get What You Want: (But If You Try Sometime, You Might Get What You Need)

The next morning, at a meeting convened with the representatives for Eventide, the free folk, Killaloo and New Harmony, Starhawk again reviewed the proposal to be presented to the Barons of New Van. It would protect existing island communities, including the Free Folk areas north, east, and west of Eventide. Sustainable forestry must be applied. When beneficial to both the free folk and the companies, labour and assistance would be provided. Both parties must agree to meet and negotiate future resource activity on the island. Starhawk added, "Failure to ratify an agreement or adhere to its tenets will result in a concentrated campaign to disrupt, disable and stop logging operations on the island." She was optimistic the caveat would not be needed.

Boris informed the Barons that a delegation from the island would meet with them. Starhawk and Richard prepared to leave for New Van that same day. As they left the harbour, they saw the work crews rebuilding the dock. That same morning the fleet of sailboats set sail to return for their home on Long Point. Proudly beside the eagle flags of Ahana's nation were the red carnations of New Harmony. The New Van contingent would stay on a few days longer. It seemed only fair that since they tore the docks down, they should help to rebuild them. But they were very proud of what they had done. Robert and Inga decided to return to New Van with them. There was a People's March for which to prepare. He and Inga looked forward to visiting their old haunts. Besides, with Anita gone, Stephen would need some cheering up.

The free folk and Killaloo campers were busy packing up. When necessary, tents were quite adequate, but they missed their homes and families. At Naomi's tent, Sam was busy loading the horses with their packs. Naomi was petting Frodo. She was happy Sam had decided to spend the summer in Killaloo. Barney was also pleased, and promised Sam he would earn his keep.

There was one member of Killaloo who was not returning: Richard had spent his free time with Jana after the siege. Before he left for New Van, he asked her to stay in Eventide. Jana said yes. When he returned, they would build their friendship. Sandra was pleased.

Gab, Adam, and Cody said their goodbyes to resume their duties as wanderers. The island relied on them to spread the news and bring connection to its citizens.

Back at Doug and Sandra's, it was busy. Jana's news was wonderful. Isla and Suzanne were busy writing. Charles and Angela, all packed and ready for the road said their goodbyes. It had been one year since Angela brought Charles the book. A year since Charles left the only home he had ever known. He was going home to Earthborn with his soul mate. Summer in Earthborn was like no other anywhere and he would be there.

New Van: The Monster

The streets of New Van were quiet. After dusk, a curfew was in effect. Fearing an insurgence after the Eventide incident, the militias were on full alert. Any disruption—even minor—was contained. Many young men and women had been arrested and were being held in detention centres throughout the city.

Robert and Inga arrived earlier in the day with the first group from Eventide to return and were now safe behind dorm doors. Cedric filled them in on the events of the past two days. The New Life community had been raided by militia in the name of security and 'keeping the peace.' Activists were detained, and many had not been seen since. Support for their release was being solicited by Father Raymond.

Cedric was almost in tears, "Many of us broke curfew last night. There were a hundred of us or more. There was no warning. Mostly with clubs, the militia busted heads and left us bloodied in the street. These are dark times. It's the hatred I don't understand. We are not a threat."

Inga asked about her friends and then looked at Cedric and said, "Are you alright, my dear friend?" She held him close.

"Life is often hard, at best," he said. "We are being divided by fear. I am afraid the anger of some of our comrades will bring them even more harm. The arsenals of the powerful contain weapons we cannot confront."

"Some folk, the panthers, have been protecting their enclaves by shadowing the militia. They are also feeding and housing their people. The militia will clamp down soon."

Robert could not believe what he had witnessed. "Cedric, I don't understand. What has changed since I have been gone?"

Cedric explained, "Kirk and his reporters have been writing stories in the 'Phoenix' about the inequities in our city. Revealing the bully tactics of the private police has not been well received. Posters have been appearing on campus about the March for Justice and Peace to be held June 1st. The status quo is threatened, and they are afraid.

"Kirk is the editor of the student newspaper," said Inga. He is a friend and fellow conspirator."

Cedric added, "I fear the militia will not long be waiting to shut him down, and more. He explained, "The powers that be are cautious about coming on campus. After all, their children go to school here. But they will not be deterred for long."

Days passed. When Stephen and John arrived, they were shocked by recent developments. Some of the activists had been released but many had not been seen and their location was unknown. Stephen had connections and was busy doing what he could.

Robert helped where he could and the next day he walked to the co-operative where Inga was a member. He would help and he did not want her walking home alone. He passed through the Latin quarter and the Black streets of New Van. There was a gay enclave, as well, but it was on the east side. He tried to fathom why these divisions existed. The concept of divisions by race and colour and sexual orientation was beyond reason. Yet it existed here. Only the native peoples seemed absent from the mosaic. Many had migrated to the island.

On the street's edge sat a man who spoke to Robert. "Hello, my man," he said. "I could use the company and maybe a coin or two for food." Robert noticed he was wearing a threadbare militia jacket. Robert handed him some coin.

"Why are you here?" he asked. The veteran's story was short. He was not looking for pity. He had fallen on hard times, was mostly what he said.

Then his eyes brightened, and he asked Robert, "Would you come with me? I would like to take you to my favourite place."

Robert did not hesitate, "I would be honoured. Lead the way."

Not two blocks away, he pointed to the bridge where he said he kept his tent. One block more, and they stood in front of an old church. "We enter here," he said. Through two big doors, they saw the altar, and on the side, many candles, some lit and some not.

Robert and his companion approached the altar. "Say your prayer and then light your candle," said the vet. "It will give you some peace."

As directed, Robert followed the vet. The soft light of the candles, and the aura of the ceilings that approached the sky, affected him. Mostly, he was awed by the faith and hope he saw in his new friend's eyes. They both lit their candles. He found peace here from demons Robert could not even imagine. When they left the church, Robert asked the man if he would come with him. He would find him a home. The man declined the offer and thanked Robert for his companionship.

When Robert arrived at the co-op, he found a buzz of activity. All manner of food goods was being delivered and sorted by a multitude of members and volunteers. He pitched in. People came and went, taking much needed food back to families in need. Some hours later, he and Inga finished their work and left for home as well. The streets were quiet, and curfew was less than an hour away. The silence was eerie.

In a large room on campus, Professor Racheal Phidd and several of her colleagues were addressing a large crowd of students. She was giving fair warning, "If we publish the 'Framework for Local Government,' we will be branded as agitators and may be arrested or worse."

In the room sat students—most of whom had not known hard times. They were idealists, young and eager to build a better place to live for others. Most could not imagine this chaos might happen. Many were just there for the excitement.

The vote was taken to publish. It passed. Tomorrow, the manifesto would be on the streets. One student covered his eyes in sadness. He came from a family barely able to afford his tuition. To cover expenses, he worked as much as he attended classes. He said to the fellow beside him, "I came for an education. I did not sign up for this." The student beside him didn't understand.

The churches still provided meals to needy patrons. In these times they were even more needed. Barbara was busy at the kitchen near New Life. A shelter was nearby, and an addiction help centre called Kool-Aid was busy next door. Many of their patrons were young and lost in the large city. Addiction and exploitation were part of life. As they could, volunteers helped those in need.

At the Black Swan coffee house people still gathered to forget their troubles, listen to great music and dream of better times to come. As Rose was quick to add, "The food is good and the company even better."

Robert, Inga, and the rest of the dorm crew arrived in time to find seats with Rose, her partner, and friends. Time had obviously passed. Rose was very big, and her baby could not be long coming. She was ready and looking forward to being a new mother. "I'm hungry," she said. "Let's order."

Stephen recommended the borscht. Robert said he would try it. When delivered to the table, Robert took his first bite. Rather than make a rash judgment he tried another. Then he looked at Stephen and said, "It must be an acquired taste." Rose leaned over and assured him that he was not alone in his assessment.

Cedric took the stage with Richard. They began to recite from their favourite bard. Hamlet's soliloquy was haunting in this time of uncertainty. Some light moments from A Midsummer Night's Dream raised the audience spirits. The guitars came out and John and Robert joined them. One of Cedric's songs concluded the set. It was called, 'We're Not Gonna Take It.' No one knew Who wrote it.

At the evening's end, Cedric wished everyone a safe road home. The curfew was in effect and care was needed. He left them with a few of Shakespeare's words:

"Trust in the Father.
Trust in your Brother
Trust in yourself
and in each other."

The patrons began to leave. They passed the sign at the door: 'Give What You Can'.

The next day the 'Framework for Local Government' was published in The Phoenix. That afternoon the presses were smashed, and the offices of The Phoenix destroyed.

On the deck of the ferry, Starhawk and Richard stood looking back at the harbour. Their meetings with the Barons were not amicable, but in the end, an agreement was made for one season.

The dock in Eventide was repaired, and the loggers would return. Richard was happy with the outcome but feared for the future. There were no guarantees new talks would begin in the fall.

PART 5:

Life is a Carnival

Oh, the comfort-
The inexpressible comfort of feeling safe with a person-
Having neither to weigh thoughts nor measure words,
By pouring them all right out, just as they are,
Chaff and grain together,
Certain that a faithful hand will take & sift them,
Keep what is worth keeping, & then with a breath of kindness
Blow the rest away.

Dinah Craik

Earthborn: When I Was Young

The road to Earthborn was quiet. It was May and the island was blooming. The great pines and magnificent cedars dominated the landscape. In the meadows and on the rock faces, colourful bushes of red and yellow burst forth. In the meadows and by the streams, wildflowers in blue, white, and bright yellow held forth. Best of all were the grand maple groves. Charles was still convinced that the many rivers they forded were all just one pesky stream winding back and forth throughout the land.

After the tumult in Eventide in mid April, Angela and Charles were eager to be on the road. Charles had not seen his childhood home for almost a year. Angela was just glad to be travelling again. As much as she loved the idea of home, she was also very comfortable on the trails of her island. Even the horses seemed to sense they were returning home. Carrot, their trusty donkey, seemed to have a lighter step as they approached the great wood.

Angela admired her man riding beside her, his light brown hair blowing in the wind. Out of his village paradise, she had taken a boy and introduced him to the big wide world. Now he was a man, her husband and soulmate. He turned toward her, as if knowing her thoughts, and smiled.

"Your blue eyes bewitched me from the moment we met, and they still do," Charles spoke. "I would follow you anywhere, my love. I am so glad you are in my dream." Their eyes met and the world seemed to stop.

"I will always be in your dream if you will always be in mine," Angela answered.

Soon the windmills could be seen in the distance. The woods opened to reveal the village of Earthborn. In the fields, green sprouts were seen poking out of the soil. The orchards were in full bloom. By the stream, the mill wheel was turning. Near the town square, Charles could see Sam's house with its rose garden and Sam's father sitting on the porch. In the space where an ash grove once stood, several new cottages had appeared. The shops were busy. Over by the big maple where Charles had sat with Robert and Isla, townsfolk were gathered. Tom held a book and was reading to his listeners. Both Charles and Angela savoured the moment, knowing it would soon be interrupted. Charles could feel the world he loved so much going about its daily routines. People living their lives, mindful of a reality based on mutual respect and dignity. People living values that recognized the needs of the soul. A community where love of life, where care for body and mind, takes precedence over all else. A place where 'do no harm and care for one another' has meaning. "Earthborn's secrets are real and worth sharing," thought Charles.

Carrot, the donkey, saw Mary and brayed loud enough to alert everyone around. Tom and his fellow villagers came running, with Mary and Star leading the way. Raven was not far behind. The road was soon crowded with every citizen who could see and hear the commotion. Charles and Angela were home. Little Mary jumped into Charles' arms and hugged and kissed him until he lost his balance and the two of them landed on the ground and laughed and laughed. Tom embraced Angela, and Darla hugged her, and so did just about everyone else. Charles' parents soon arrived and rescued their son from Mary to welcome him home. Even the newcomers from New Harmony joined in the reunion. Raven, who was a year older now, took the horses to Charles' home, and Mary pulled Carrot, who was stubborn as a mule.

In a while, the road cleared, and folks went back about their business—although the business would now be to get ready for a welcoming home party. "It is a good time for a party," thought Tom. His wife agreed. Raven helped Charles and his father unpack the bags, and Raven bedded the horses. Mary lost interest in

Carrot, and Star settled her in her stall. Charles' mother had a lot of catching up to do.

Early next morning, Charles woke from a deep and comfortable sleep that left him refreshed and ready to greet the day. "Waking is such a wonderful thing," thought Charles. "The sun is rising in the eastern sky. Blue sky in the morning—it's the beginning of a beautiful day." Out the window, he saw the robin get the worm and he cried, "Hello world, here I come."

Next to him, a sleepy blue-eyed beauty with auburn hair arose from her pillow and cried, "What are you doing? It's six o'clock in the morning and the chickens aren't even awake!" Then she laughed and wrapped her arms around her early morning riser. Without hesitation, Charles began to sing,

"The sun is rising over the hills. The rays are peeking through the blinds.

We should rise and greet the morning, But I just want to stay in here with you." He held her in his arms and kissed her gently on the lips. With the warmth of her breasts on his chest and their legs intertwined, Charles reassessed the situation and sang,

"I don't want to go. Just want to stay in here with you.

To look into your eyes and see the morning dew.

I just want to stay in here with you." They pulled down the blinds. Angela straddled her man and said, "Where were you planning to go without saying good morning to me?"

Charles was twenty-four, and the world seemed to be as good as it could get.

Some time later, Charles resumed his morning routine. This new addition was definitely worth keeping. Washing was a treat, as they felt the warm water on their backs, dried themselves in the morning sun, and dressed in the clothes they had set out the night before. Breakfast was taken with family and friends as it had always been.

Under the grand maple, Tom and Darla and a few elders met with Charles that morning. There was so much to talk about that no one quite knew where to begin. The whereabouts of Isla, Robert, and now Sam was first on the list.

Charles recounted the stand-off in Eventide. As he told his listeners the story of the folding docks, the Native armada and all the people who made it all possible, there was not a whisper. In the telling, he realized how attached he had become to that outside world and its people. Charles was asked many questions about the conflict.

He answered, "Starhawk and Richard, our friends in Eventide, are negotiating an arrangement to protect the people and the resources of our island." He explained how the Barons in the city controlled the forests and the fisheries up and down the coast. He assured them that Earthborn had many allies who were ready to protect their home. He concluded, "We have many friends in many places."

As for Robert and Inga, he explained, "They were staying in the city of New Van and participating in a great march to bring reforms and a new government for the people." He began to recite some details, but reconsidered. Instead he added, "I expect they will be coming home soon." That placated his audience. "News of that event is at least a month away, and perhaps Robert and Inga will bring it."

They were saddened to hear that Isla and Suzanne would not be returning soon to Earthborn. They were joining Starhawk on her journey home to Morningstar. Tom and Darla looked forward to Isla's poetry and Suzanne's writings when they finally did come home.

Saving the story of Sam and Frodo for the second last update, Charles happily told them all about Sam's adventures. Wide-eyed and eager, Sam had embraced the new world.

Charles laughed, "Sam almost fainted when he met all of these characters he was told about. He truly found a bond with the folk from Killaloo. One of the free folk, Quiet Sue, had a soft spot for Sam and introduced him to all of her friends." The audience was hooked. "Cody, who you all know, played matchmaker and pushed Sam into a very lovely Killaloo girl named Naomi. Their dance at the Eventide celebration sealed the deal, and Sam is on his way to Killaloo for the summer. Have no fear: Frodo is still by his side, wagging his oversized tail."

Tom interjected, "And you have no personal news to impart?" They all waited for Charles to speak.

With a wee bit of a blush Charles said, "Angela and I took vows in the Cathedral Forest. It is a sacred place and we exchanged sacred vows of marriage. We cannot wait to say them amidst our 'family' here." The audience aahed and laughed and congratulated Charles.

"There must be more. You have been away for one whole year," said Darla.

And so, Charles told the tales of their adventure to Windmill Valley. He talked of his dear friend John and their walks in the woods with Shanda, the border collie. He talked of how Angela found her home with Rita, her new 'Mom.'

Then he burst out laughing with excitement, "We are building a house. It will be shaped like an A and sit by a stream. And we will build a boat to row on the lake nearby."

The group all had one more question. In unison they asked, "Where will this house be built?"

At that moment, a smiling blue-eyed woman appeared and answered the question. She said, "In Windmill Valley, not far from Killaloo. And we hope you all will visit." Everyone stood and congratulated the newest couple in the community of Earthborn.

Darla then spoke for everyone there, "It's time for another wedding."

Charles and Angela spent their time sharing in the maintenance of their community. Much time was spent just living life. As the spring days were spent and became the early days of summer, Charles held the wonders of this place in his heart. He pointedly examined how and why Earthborn worked. He learned what made it work, how community was built, and the ways obstacles were overcome. He noted how decisions were made, what details made this possible and what obstacles needed to be avoided. He compared Earthborn to the places he had seen, and logged the similarities and the differences. Knowing what factors created this village and sustained it was essential for building community elsewhere.

Of particular interest were the new inhabitants of his village. The immigrants from New Harmony had much to teach him. They came from a large very progressive city. Their insights were invaluable to compare what they left behind to what they now found in Earthborn. Charles knew in his heart that he would need this information in his future.

Eventide: All I Really Want to Do

Into the new dock came the New Van ferry. On the shore were waiting Isla and Suzanne. Beside them stood Jana, in a beautiful new dress she and Sandra had just sewed. Not far from her stood Douglas and Sandra. The passengers began to unload. First off came Starhawk and Richard, eager to see their friends. Richard held a bouquet of flowers. He ran to Jana and held her tight. The others welcomed Starhawk. What became of the talks in the city could wait. It was time for welcomes and homecomings.

The last debarkation was a young couple with two young children and a lot of luggage.

That evening, everyone gathered at Doug and Sandra's home. Richard assured everyone that most of the conditions were met to protect the island and its settlements for at least one season. He and Starhawk both felt there was some hope for a good future. The details were being distributed by wanderers already. Starhawk, Isla and Suzanne would also deliver the news on their way home to Morningstar.

With faces glowing, Richard and Jana announced they had found a house not far from Doug and Sandra. They would be busy setting up their new home. Richard was quite busy with his new job as chief organizer for the free folk and unofficial mayor of Eventide. In a makeshift shop on Main Street, Jana had set up a nurse's station, and was already busy.

Isla and Suzanne were already packed and eager to return to Morningstar. Suzanne expected it would be one week of travel ahead of them. She missed her mother, Emma, her home, and her beloved library. Isla, too, was looking forward to being in Morningstar again.

Across town in his living quarters, Boris was meeting with his newest recruit. He had offered Michael a job in April, and Michael had accepted. He had reservations about joining the militia again, but with reassurances from Boris and some discussions with Richard, he decided it would be good for his family, and hopefully he could contribute to the well-being of his new town.

"They are a good lot, all in all, and they have respect for their fellow townsfolk now," said Boris. He handed Michael an ale and sat across from him. "The dock conflict could have been much worse, and I expect there may be more unrest," said Boris, "But there is some time to make this work."

Michael responded, "I have respect for law and order; I always have. I also value human life and recognize the harsh realities in which we live. The law must be fair and balanced."

"No promises, my man, but I, too, have a new respect for my neighbours," Boris said. From that point on, it was small talk. Boris didn't have this rapport with his other men, but he broke the rule with Michael. His friend Robert and Richard both vouched for Michael's loyalty. What happened at the docks had changed Boris. His men were saved by the same men and women who his men had beaten up. Michael was one of the first to help.

Boris set the family up in a nice duplex. Michael made a point to get to know his fellow militiamen. He felt right about his decision to come to Eventide. Already, his wife Anna had met Jana, and they had hit it off right away. He even thought it would be great if Richard and Jana decided to start their own family one day. He could use another father with whom to share, as a father of two young girls himself.

It was May, and Eventide became a busy port again. Employment was full. In the east end, the sawmill was gearing up to full production. This was Douglas' busy time. The fish plant was already at capacity, as the boats came in with salmon to be salted and dried. The free folk had kept their side of the bargain and were assisting operations. The loggers honoured the restrictions in the agreement. For now, the militia's main concern was drunken loggers. That suited Boris to a tee, and Michael proved an excellent addition to his squad.

One night a week in the community hall, the locals gathered to enjoy the music, share food and drink, and enjoy the company of their neighbours. Doug was the lead singer for The Eventide Conspiracy, a band of renown, if only in Eventide. Sandra found a table for herself and Jana. When Michael and his wife arrived, Sandra ushered them over.

At the next table sat Boris and a few of his mates. He had started attending village activities since the dock conflict. Sandra made a point to go to his table and introduce him to her friends.

Back at her spot, a bottle of wine and home-baked snacks were being placed upon the table.

Michael's wife said, "These are for you, Sandra and Jana, for welcoming my family. We have had some hard times, and you have made these few days so wonderful for us."

"Eventide does not have much, but we have each other," smiled Sandra, "And you are part of us now."

At the head of the table, Jana was almost in tears. She held Anna's hand and said, "This place has a magical touch. You are not the first person to find happiness in Eventide." The band played one of their favourites and the dance floor was filling.

Boris came to the table and asked Anna for a dance. Michael smiled and asked Sandra to dance with him. Still at the table, Jana surveyed the room full of people—her people—and smiled. Richard was doing his guitar solo, and smiled down at her. She said to herself, "I am truly blessed."

There were no drunken loggers this night, and the moon was large over the bay. Across the water, the city of New Van was preparing for its day. June 1st was only days away and the city was preparing to march.

New Van: Your Time Is Gonna Come

New Life Community was the nerve centre of the march. Very early, organizers gathered, although there was little, now, for them to do. By ten a.m. June 1st, the crowds started coming. It was a three-mile walk to Candlestick Park and the streets were full. They were young and they were old and there were many in-between. They kept coming, and the marchers moved slowly along the route. It was too late to have second thoughts. Once in the crowd, you were no longer alone.

There were moments when a voice chanted 'We shall overcome' and the crowd answered, "We shall overcome someday." The singing was joyful. The sheer experience of thousands of souls sharing with one another was sometimes overwhelming. For the first time in months, there was no fear. There was only joy and purpose. We were so many.

The militia watched and held their distance.

There was hugging and laughing and crying with friends, family, and people who had never met before. At times, a person would stop walking and just marvel at the mass of humanity moving in one direction. David was one of those. He didn't even come from New Van. He picked one incredible time to be there. It was very 'far out.' He folded a poster from a lamppost and put it in his pocket for safekeeping.

And the militia watched and held their distance.

It took hours for the multitude of people to gather in the park. On the ocean's edge, the view was surreal as the speeches began. Father Raymond took the stage and he looked over thousands of faces.

What was said that afternoon was not important. It was what was felt that mattered. The messages of hope and the promise of a better future to come were what mattered. The knowledge that you were not alone anymore was what remained after everyone went home and resumed their lives.

Father Raymond announced plans to hold elections in the autumn for a city mayor and council to represent all of the people. He spoke with feeling and with conviction, "The people of New Van will begin to guide their own future."

As the park emptied, the men of the militias watched and held their distance. Some in the crowd gave them flowers and raised their hand with their fingers split in vees. A young girl with flowers in her hair sang, "All we are saying is give peace a chance."

In a tiny apartment with her proud husband and a midwife, Rose was holding her newborn baby. She was a mother and a new life was born this day. She called her baby June. It was June and this was her first child. The Black Swan Conspiracy was growing. The conspiracy for peace was alive and well.

New Van: Father and Son

Three days after the march, Stephen hopped the trolley and rode to his parents' home north of the city. So much had happened in the past two months. He had kept his promise and kept his father up-to-date on all developments, both in Eventide and in New Van. On arrival, the welcome was almost cordial, and Mr. Cunniff and his son sat down in his office.

"First of all, I would like to thank you for your restraint and your consideration of the issues," said Stephen in complete sincerity. He paused and began again, but was stopped by his father's response.

"Relax, son," his father interjected, "I am aware of your efforts to find compromise here. I am also aware that the world is changing. Besides, I have every expectation that you will take charge of my holdings perhaps sooner than I might have thought. I have talked with Scott and the others, and we have a proposal for you." Stephen was speechless. He just listened.

James continued, "Our consortium has prospects in many sectors of this coast. It seems we can prosper through cooperation, perhaps, better than by mere force. After Eventide, it is also obvious there are other interests in play with considerable reach." His father obviously found these revelations hard to admit, and even harder to accept.

"Peter Scott and I have convinced the others, with a lot of arm twisting, to hire you as our chief negotiator this fall. We will agree to sit down with the island representatives to establish a way forward. You will by no means have free reign. Peter's daughter Kate will be your second. As you know, she is far more aligned with our thinking than you." With that, he became silent.

Stephen could not believe what he had just heard. But then again, he could. His father was a good man and he would give his son every opportunity to succeed.

"I will accept the job with humility and thanks, Dad. I will make you proud," he said, and vowed to himself to do everything in his power to make it so.

His father was smiling, in a rare show of emotion. "As Peter Scott would say, 'Don't screw up.'" Almost as an afterthought, he said, "As for that local government proposal, we'll see how it evolves."

On his way home, excited and relieved, Stephen said out loud, "I am going to learn to sail." He would spend the summer in New Harmony. His teacher had promised him the premium lesson package.

Morningstar: Tangled up in Blue

Five days in, the three women could feel their home over the horizon. They had skirted Lake Couchiching, and their steps became lighter. In one more day they would be on the well-worn trail to their beloved village. May was a pretty month, even if it was a little wet. There had been rain, but Suzanne and Starhawk knew free folk throughout the region who sheltered them for the nights. Up ahead was the beautiful escarpment which looked over the northeastern horizon. Farther than one could see were the wilds. Settled between the mountains and the sea was the land still not well travelled, and still isolated from the islander people.

Starhawk stood eyeing the far lands, "Someday we will meet the peoples of those reaches. It may be sooner than we think." Her companions wondered what Starhawk imagined.

Suzanne mused, "Perhaps we should wander that way someday when we are in need of a new adventure. It does not look that far away."

Isla kissed her on the cheek and noted, "Perhaps we should finish this journey, first, before planning the next." Both Starhawk and Suzanne thought that to be a good plan.

With journals full and in their packs, the three ladies of the woods arrived in Morningstar two days later. Nestled in the woods beside the river, houses of red and white, blue, and some yellow, appeared before them. The closer they came, they could see the little shops, the water tower, and the mill. It was not long before the villagers appeared—as if by magic—to welcome them home.

From around the corner of the dead-end street, Mother Emma ran with open arms. Tired and road weary, the three women were ready for a hot bath and a well-deserved rock in the lounge chair under the beech tree by the river. But that could wait. Emma led them to the cafe so everyone could hear, and waited for their stories.

Much later, after promises were made to read their journals and recite Isla's poetry, the weary wanderers retired. Suzanne and Isla went home to their little cottage full of memories and books and their comfortable bed. Emma hustled Starhawk back to her house. Whether Starhawk got any rest is in doubt. Emma was eager to hear everything Starhawk had to tell.

In the lazy days of late May and June, the couple settled into a routine which seemed to work even for Suzanne's mother. Rather of a single mind, Emma was expecting that her girls would spend most of their time working in the library and drinking tea with their mother. The compromise saw Suzanne and Isla in the library most mornings after their morning yoga meditation. In the afternoons, they compiled their notes and prepared the next book. It was time to record new history.

At dusk, they often walked the labyrinth. Isla sat on the small bench washing her feet in the fresh bubbling water of the stream. The walkway was sided by the stream, a grove of oak trees, and a garden of roses. She always prayed to the gods of nature before beginning her meditation.

Isla chanted, "Thank you, Gaia, for the blessings of this day. I will cherish you, as I know you cherish your children." She walked the paths in quiet as the labyrinth took her deep into a restful place where all of life's challenges melted away. She became a mote in god's eye: A pebble in a grand canyon.

As Suzanne browsed her notes, she marvelled at the change she had experienced around her. "Only a year ago," she realized, "We decided to reveal the secret of Earthborn. The Book was written, and is now in every part of our little world." She held her notes on Eventide, "Our isolated island is now the centre of a conflict which has challenged the human race since the beginning." She wondered how the next chapter would unfold.

Then she smiled. "Amidst all the conflicts of our existence, there is always one thread which is woven throughout the tapestry of life. It is human relationships which can be found in that thread. It is love and human kindness that always find a way to make the sun shine and our frowns turn into smiles. Love is all you need."

She looked over at Isla, lounging on the couch, reading a book by Kahil Gibran. She sighed a grateful sigh, "Love is all you need."

Killaloo: I'm Going to the Country

"Can you believe this, Frodo? Here we are in the middle of the country, with people we just met, having the time of our lives," said Sam. He was looking into the eyes of his furry friend in the middle of a field, surrounded by a herd of goats.

From over a wall made of stones came a young lady wearing a full-length dress of cotton in as many colours as a rainbow. "What are you doing out here?" she asked. He was a vision to behold, lying on the ground hugging his dog. And so was she.

"I am telling my friend that I must be living in a dream," said Sam with a big grin.

"And what is Frodo telling you?" laughed Naomi.

Sam was very quick to answer, "Perhaps you should ask him yourself." Naomi gave up and joined her two friends rolling in the grass. From a safe distance, the goats just watched in amazement. At least that's what Sam thought. Naomi was sure he spoke fluent 'goat' as well as 'bark.'

Gab's parents had an extra room and were quick to invite Sam to stay with them. They missed their wandering son and were very pleased when Sam arrived with his sidekick Frodo. To earn his keep Sam assisted Barney and earned 'money' for doing much of the same kinds of work as he did in Earthborn. He was also very helpful to Gab's parents who grew a large garden and kept chickens and goats. With the chickens Frodo was expected to keep his distance. 'The Folks,' as Sam now called his adopted parents, had an old dog who had died not long before. Frodo filled the void just fine.

One of Sam's jobs was hoeing the 'crop'. The Killaloo folk rather liked their 'crops'. The pretty green weeds grew seven feet tall he was told. At three feet now, he looked forward to full growth. Always eager to learn, Sam helped the farmers get rid of the male plants so that the female plants would be potent and without seeds. Fertilizing was an art. Sheep manure tea was a popular blend. There were different kinds of weed and harvest was a very precise time to be calculated for preferred results. Apparently, island bud was in great demand in New Van. Great care was taken to produce quality weed. It was a matter of pride.

After a few weeks Sam became quite knowledgeable of his new community. It was a lot messier than Earthborn. There were well-established communes that shared everything—including each other. Then there were the solitary souls who hid in the hills and were rarely seen. Many were just ordinary folk who lived on small acreages and were as self sufficient as they could be. Some held strict religious beliefs. Others worshipped amanita mushrooms and L. Ron Hubbard. There was an architect who built herself a geodesic dome. There were even a few who believed God had already returned to earth and we were all capable of being her realization. A tall lanky fellow with a strong arm just liked baseball and trout fishing.

Some of them were weak and some were strong. Some worked hard and some didn't. Many were troubled and lived with their demons. Others were innocents looking for a safer world. And everyone lived there for a reason. And everyone had read The Lord of the Rings. But, as Sam soon learned, "We are all children of the universe and we all have a right to be here." It made Sam feel good to believe that. It made Killaloo a very special place.

Going to the Fair: Sugar Mountain

Perhaps the best time of year for the free folk was the Killaloo Craft Fair. Every July, the people of the communes rode up en masse. The solitary souls appeared like magic. The ordinary people just came. And the tall lanky fellow was there to play ball, not softball, but hardball the real game. Stages were built and stalls created for every kind of craft which humans can imagine.

Sam arrived with his girl by his side. He did think she was pretty in those long cotton dresses. As he surveyed the field full of everything he could imagine, Sam was just elated. Naomi had more fun watching Sam than doing whatever was to be done. Sam dragged Naomi over to the first booth. A tall, curly-haired man was offering head massages.

"Well," said Sam, "This is a must do." He sat on the wooden stool and Curly—the man's nickname—began to run his fingers through Sam's silky locks. "It's heaven," said Sam, "Pure heaven." When he was completely relaxed, Sam thanked Curly and dragged Naomi to the next activity. "You really must learn how to do that, Naomi," he smiled.

Before them was an array of silver necklaces and earrings and broaches, all handcrafted from silver. The artist was a wispy beauty with long flowing hair, and she moved and spoke like a fairy from an ancient tale. For Naomi, Sam bought a silver necklace and placed it around her neck. She was enchanting.

"You are a vision, my love. A vision of perfection," he said with passion. Naomi just smiled and thanked him for this gift. She was bursting with happiness.

With no time to waste, Sam headed for the baker's table. "Chelsea buns!" he cried. "Have you tasted these, Naomi? They are the best in the world, and the world is getting bigger every day."

It was Naomi's turn to lead the way. The table held wool sweaters of deep green and blue. They came from the farm just down the road. She had Sam pick his favourite and she purchased it with money made from her new job at the general store.

In his time away from Earthborn, Sam had acquired a taste for bacon. The butcher had a booth just down the way. "This is so great," said Sam. "Look! The blacksmith is here, and a masseuse. Goat cheese over there. That fellow makes guitars and mandolins." He sighed, "Would Robert love one of those."

"That's it," laughed Naomi. "We are going to the stage. The music is great. Let's listen for awhile." The band on stage played what they called folk rock. Sam decided the song being sung must have been written for his sweetheart. It was called Brown-eyed Girl.

Across the breeze came a sweet scent that filled the air. In the crowd gathered in front of the stage, a number of lit cylinders they called joints were circulating. Most patrons were taking a toke and then passing it on. Back in Eventide, Sam had experienced this ritual at the campfire and found it quite enjoyable. He took a toke, and another for good measure, and passed it to Naomi. Naomi had not tried it before, but trusted Sam and took a wee toke.

Several songs later and a few tokes to the wind, Sam and Naomi were singing and laughing and getting very hungry. Sam could stand it no longer. He cried, "I need bacon. Bacon and Chelsea buns and cheese." It was fun, and the couple found some bacon on a bun, cheese, and to top it all off, one more Chelsea bun.

Hand in hand, they walked the fairgrounds greeting new friends and experiencing the many wares the free folk had to offer. Later that afternoon, they watched the hardball game on the playing field. That evening on their blanket, on a knoll near the stage, they watched the stars as the band played Ride Me High.

Sam kissed his girl, looked into her soft brown eyes, and said, "I'm still hungry." They both laughed and held each other close. Frodo curled up on the blanket and went fast to sleep. It had been a busy day.

Woodstock: Peace, Love and Music

The semi-annual caravan to the island was almost there. Leading their ragtag group from the city, Abdul and Flower arrived at their chosen spot in early afternoon. It was the summer solstice, and the stars and moon and sun, and whatever else, were aligned perfectly. Abdul, a strong Aries, and his Gemini wife thanked the stars and the moon and everything else for their safe journey. His followers set up camp on the edges of a large meadow. In the centre, they set up a large pyre of wood stocks for the 'festival of peace, love and music' to come.

Flower had studied the ancient rituals of the past and was intent on recreating them in the present. She appraised her encampment and was pleased. The small stage stood in one corner, with the ocean as its backdrop. The tents were nestled near each other with full view of the stage and the wood stock pyre in the centre. In the open spaces, everyone could dance.

Sitting on his rock, already stark naked, Abdul looked over the vast channel at the mountains beyond. 'Woodstock,' named after the great bonfire to come, was extra special this year. Soon, elections would be held to elect the first local government in New Van. Its power would be very limited at first, but it would be the first step on a long road forward.

Abdul took Flower's hand as she sat down beside him. He expressed his thoughts, "We are celebrating an awakening, my love. Our people are finding their voice. Our people can feel the power of 'us.'" Flower simply replied, "The power of peace, love and music." They congratulated each other for picking such a fine name for their celebration.

And then, out of nowhere, people began to appear. Tents began to grow in the woods. People just kept arriving with sleeping bags and provisions to last their stay. Some even brought firewood.

Before the afternoon was gone, the party was three times the size it had started, and people were still coming.

A tall, young man with fire in his eyes and a heart as big as the sun found Abdul and announced, "We're here. I invited every human being I met in my travels—including a few animals. And would you believe, they are all coming."

"We are so glad to see you all, Gab," said Flower. "Although we do need to give you a new name, my boy. How about 'MacDuff?'"

Gab repeated his new name. "MacDuff! It suits me just fine," he answered. So, MacDuff sat cross-legged on another rock overlooking the ocean. "By the way, Cody should be along anytime with even more recruits."

"This conspiracy thing might have some meaning to it, after all," thought Abdul as he viewed the mass of humanity joining his party.

Into the night the festival grew and endured. The fire gave them warmth and their time together gave them strength for the future. There were enough musicians to keep the music going all night. In the air was a faint scent of island bud. In the morning, it was breakfast for five hundred souls.

Three days later, everyone went home.

Earthborn: Share the Land

The warm sunny days of July had come to the island. In Earthborn, young men and women were busy building a stage and a dance floor in the meadow just on the edge of the village. Raven proudly surveyed the new tents they had erected in the glade. The large open dining tent was occupied by a small herd of sheep taking respite from the sun. The chairs and tables had arrived, and Raven was eager to set them up.

"Shoo, shoo, shoo," cried Raven, as he did everything in his power to get the lazy animals out of his working area. Some bystanders were laughing at the battle of wills being waged between Raven and a very large ewe.

From the village, a group of women carried colourful linens out to the big tent. In the laughter, they joined, until Raven lifted his hands and cried, "I give up, you win." He helped the girls unload the fabrics onto a table. "For a very small village, we seem to have a lot of extra tables and chairs," he commented. It was a curious fact that two weddings had occurred here in the recent past, and not a tent was pitched.

A week before the wedding, Angela was escorted to Tom and Darla's. Darla claimed it was tradition to separate the bride and the groom prior to the wedding. Darla stood firm, and who was Angela to question tradition. Standing in the den, Angela was a vision wearing her new gown. Darla was hemming the full-length dress and chatting idly.

"Have you seen our meadow lately, Darla?" asked Angela. What was a week ago a field of wildflowers is now a tent city."

Darla smiled as she sewed the next stitch. "Yes, it is quite the transformation," she said. The door flew open, and Mary and Cherry, her friend, burst into the room.

"Hello Darla. Hello Angela. We are here to try on our dresses," laughed Mary.

Darla gave her a funny look. "You tried them on yesterday and the day before. You were both very beautiful," she said.

"I know," said Cherry.

Darla whisked them out the front door and told them to come back later. "We are very busy at the moment."

Standing to check the length again, Darla looked into Angela's bright blue eyes. In all seriousness she said, "Our quiet little village has certainly changed since you appeared on that fresh spring morning just one year ago." She adjusted the straps. "You have had quite an impact on our lives, my dear Angela."

Angela straightened and Darla could feel the tension. She held Angela's hands reassuringly and said, "You are a blessing to us all, my child. Life is change and change is a constant. You have brought to us the kind of change that is always welcome." She smiled and hugged Angela close. "You have brought us friendship and love. We have new purpose in our lives. What will happen next is blowing in the wind and I believe it will be a warm and gentle one."

Angela began to cry, "In my wildest dreams, I did not see this in my future," she spread her arms wide, "I am so blessed." With that, the fitting would have to wait. Darla put on some tea and the two of them sat in the living room waiting for it to steep.

"Darla, is there something I do not know about? I sense some secrets." asked Angela. Darla just smiled and poured the tea.

When Angela realized she would not get an answer, she mused, "I have just one wish. I wish Rita and John and my faraway friends could be here to share this wonderful time."

Darla set down her tea and said, "Yes, that would be nice."

At home, Charles was thinking about his vows. He and Angela had hardly seen one another for several days. Tom said that was tradition. In all his lifetime, Charles had never heard of such a silly tradition. When he thought about it, a lot of 'unusual' things were happening lately. Neither Gab nor Cody had been seen for over a month. There were enough tents in the glade to house half of Earthborn. Yet everyone kept saying what a nice little wedding it would be. As weddings in Earthborn always are.

Three days before the wedding, a caravan appeared from the forest. Leading the band of travellers were Robert and Inga. As tradition dictated, most of Earthborn's residents gathered to welcome the visitors.

Robert dismounted and announced, "We're here! I told you everyone would be here to greet us." He and Inga then tried to introduce their fellow travellers. Charles and Angela could not believe their eyes.

Inga smiled at an astonished Angela, "We found them along the way, and could not leave them behind." Sandra held Angela as Douglas embraced Charles.

From the group, Richard appeared with a girl on his arm. "I want you to meet Jana." No more needed to be said.

Two new faces with awed looks on their faces introduced themselves, "I'm Michael, and this is my wife Anna and our two children." He looked at Douglas and glanced around the crowd and the mythical village. "Thank you for letting us come," he said. Cedric and John just grinned and decided their introductions could wait.

A short distance away from the crowd, a young man with a knapsack sat down against the big maple. He looked quite content just taking it all in.

"Who is he?" asked Charles.

Inga giggled and responded, "We really did find him along the way and just could not leave him behind."

When everybody settled, and Raven had escorted their guests to their new quarters, Charles sat with Robert on his front porch.

"Don't act so surprised," Robert said. "The whole island knows about this wedding and most of its people would like to be here."

"Well, I am so glad you got the news, because I really need a best man," said Charles.

At the noon hour meal the following day, Angela looked west to see three riders approaching. She was already a fount of emotions, but when she saw Stephen riding up, she lost it completely. Her best friend ran to meet her with two beautiful women at his sides. Anita, Stephen's new love, and her friend Shania were greeted with no reservation.

"Oh, Stephen! Oh, Stephen!" was all she could say.

Anita held her close and whispered, "It took two of us to make up for the girl he missed."

Shortly after Stephen's arrival, Gab appeared with another cast of characters. He had a rather silly grin on his face when Robert and Charles welcomed him to the village. Darla was quick to join them.

"Has everyone arrived?" he asked innocently.

Darla pulled him off his horse and gave him a big hug. "Almost," she said in his ear.

By this time, Tom sidled up.

Gab, the wanderer, with a glint in his eye, introduced his friends, "Raymond and Barbara, please meet my dear friends, Tom and Darla."

Barbara spoke, "Please call us Abdul and Flower. This is a celebration and those are our party names. We wouldn't miss Sparkle and Rosebud's wedding for the world."

Darla, between fits of joy and laughing, took Flower's hand. "You and I are going to be very good friends. I think you have some stories to tell."

For a village that was a secret for generations, Earthborn had become a very well-known place. Tom spent a good deal of his time reassuring residents that everything was okay and a return to normal would come someday, maybe. On the night before the big event, the village was in full celebration. Earthborn's guests were having a wonderful time making new acquaintances. The residents soon realized that the big world out there had good people just like themselves.

After a fine meal, Charles sat with Stephen and Robert reminiscing about the year just past. The moon shone bright in the western sky and a warm breeze blew over the island. Fires could be seen in the meadow and the sharp sound of a fiddle and a ukulele floated on the wind. Laughter and song danced in the early evening light. Charles' mind drifted, and he could feel the greater forces at work in his world. He looked at Robert, his original merry explorer, and Stephen, his new friend and Black Swan co-conspirator. He said out loud, "Maybe there is more to this conspiracy thing than I first thought."

Stephen smiled, "Maybe there is."

Robert looked at them both, incredulous, "I never had any doubts." He raised his glass, "To the Black Swan Conspiracy and its unrelenting mission to bring peace to a weary world." The wine was good and the friends even better.

"Would you have a glass for me?" a familiar voice came from the street. Out of the twilight came a tall lanky blonde. "We are a tad late, but that dog decided to chase a rabbit." She added, "Have I missed anything?"

Cody, the wanderer, joined her friends. Charles gave up his chair and sat on the stair. He gave her a hug and said in all seriousness, "I can't thank you enough for what you have done."

"It is all in the job, my friend. But I did have a great deal of help." She took a large drink and laughed. "Our young man, Sam has become a full-fledged free folk, and is dying to see you guys, but his mom wouldn't let him out of her sight." They all laughed. "And wait for this: he has a girl." She rolled her eyes. "That's a story in itself."

"John and Rita are with Angela at Tom's. I have never seen our Angela so happy," continued Cody. "And Isla is on her way. She wouldn't miss the wedding of her first love." Charles blushed a little.

"You have performed a miracle, my friend," said Charles. Life is just one exciting adventure after another, I am convinced."

Robert could remain silent no longer. Jokingly, he said, "Inga told me life is like a box of chocolates; you never know what you're going to get. And with you for friends, you never do."

Stephen cried, "Stop! All this wisdom at once is just overwhelming." He paused and looked at Cody, "Do you know John is here? He arrived yesterday."

"I do," said Cody, "And he is going to keep me warm tonight."

The Gathering: Here Comes the Sun

Standing in the meadow, Tom inhaled Earthborn's wedding chapel. In his flowing robe, he felt the power of this place. The sun was high in the sky. The sky was a deep blue. The cedar forest in the distance enveloped the meadow. The great maple shaded the knoll where so many stories had been told. Everyone had gathered. The melodic notes of Robert's mandolin carried through the crowd.

Two very fidgety flower girls finally had permission to lead the procession to the dais. Mary looked up at Angela in her white gown and rose bouquet, and said, "You look very beautiful with flowers in your hair." Angela took a flower from her head and slipped it in her young admirer's hair.

When the time came for John, her adopted father, to leave her beside her betrothed, he said, "You are much loved, my daughter."

Tom began, "Today, the people of Earthborn welcome family from all parts of our island. Until recently, we had no past. Our present continues to inspire us, and with all of you, our future looks bright. This union and the two before this bring our two worlds together as one. We are family."

Charles held Angela's hands, "Once upon a time, a beautiful blue-eyed girl gave me a book. It read, 'When the past and future take precedence over the present, your life will change.' Well, my life has changed, and for the better. Angela, I look forward to our future together and I will love you with all my heart in the present."

Angela answered, "When I watched you from a distance, I saw a man who was special. My past had been troubled, and my future looked uncertain. With you, in the present is the only place I ever want to be."

Tom pronounced them husband and wife. A collective sigh rested over the gathering. There were papers to sign and scrolls to complete, as one more new couple took their vows in Earthborn.

The celebration was the largest anyone there had ever seen. The Eventide Conspiracy took the stage and played everyone's favourites. There was no lack of musicians. Quiet Sue was on drums and John and Robert joined in with their guitar and mandolin.

Tom and Darla shared a table with Abdul and Flower. Darla assured Flower they would be in attendance at next year's Woodstock Festival. On the dress code, Tom was still a little shaky.

Mary and Cherry quickly assumed responsibility for Michael and Anna's girls. It was likely Mary would be wearing her dress for days to come. Raven had assumed the role of chief organizer for event activities.

Robert's new song, Wagon Wheel, was a big hit. Sam preferred the slower songs. He and Naomi never left the dance floor.

Cedric announced it was time for the Bride and Groom's dance. Backed by Robert's mandolin, he sang a new poem composed by Isla. It was called 'Imagine'.

Under the stars, the 'family' became one.

Cedric, in his finest Shakespearian form, recited:

Trust in the father.

Trust in your brother

Trust in yourself and in each other.

Love is the answer to enquiring eyes.

Love is the dancer

That dances so lightly

Before your eyes.

In the next few days, Earthborn's visitors began to pack up and prepare to make their way home. Sam and Naomi were going back to Killaloo. Suzanne and Isla left early; it was a long way to Morningstar. Charles and Angela had a house to build in an aspen grove, by a stream, close to a windmill. Robert and Inga were not going anywhere. They were home.

Two weeks later, all packed with Carrot, the donkey, eager to go, Charles and Angela joined Robert and Inga by the old maple. Sitting there reading the book was a young, very innocent-looking young man with long brown hair and a knapsack.

Charles asked, "Who are you?"

Inga answered, "I remember you. We met you on our journey here."

The young man, through smiling eyes, said, "I was told of a wonderous place where people were building a new world, where there was no violence—only love and acceptance. A place that celebrated life in all of its forms. A place with only one rule, 'Care for one another and do no harm.' I wanted to see it." He stood up and said, "Hi, I'm David." He raised his hand and formed the sign of peace.

Charles could only say, "Welcome home."

PART 6:

The Field of Opportunity

Today's world requires us to accept the oneness of humanity.
In the past, isolated communities could afford to
think of one another as fundamentally separate.
Some could even exist in total isolation.
But nowadays, whatever happens in one region
eventually affects many other areas.
Within the context of our inter-dependence, self-interest
clearly lies in considering the interests of others.

His Holiness the Dalai Lama

New Van: Reason to Believe

The salmon run had just begun. The days were getting cooler and autumn was in the air. In a room at the university, Dr. Rachel Phidd, William, and Barbara were deep in discussion. On the table was The Framework for Local Government. Modifications had been made since its inception. Amendments proposed by the Barons of New Van were grudgingly accepted and incorporated into the final constitution.

William was visibly excited, "Just three days to elections," he said. We will have a local government. New Van will officially become a city."

Running for mayor was Barbara Warren, alias Flower. Her work in the New Life Community was well known. She was talented and connected to many organizations in the city. She stated, "If I am elected, I will need a great deal of support to make this work. We will start slowly, William. You will have to be patient."

Rachel, a professor of government organization, supported Barbara's warning. "We will require the tacit support of the Barons and their willingness to invest their wealth for the greater good." She continued, "The transfer of security services from the militias to a local police force will be difficult and slow. 'To Serve and Protect' is not a mantra easily assumed."

Running as a councillor, William had worked tirelessly, knocking on doors and making speeches. The council would be a mix of activists like William, and those less eager for change. The Barons had insisted upon the right of veto on a number of aspects to be incorporated into the new structure. William asserted, "There is no if. I will be elected, and I will be patient. At least I will try. Patience is not a common word in my vocabulary."

Rachel assured her colleagues, "Even with the amendments, we have an opportunity here to make a very real difference as we go forward."

Barbara reminded her colleagues of the long road leading to this day. I believe the Black Swan Conspiracy is alive and well, and our New Life community will celebrate."

Three days later, Barbara Warren became Mayor of New Van. William was one of the city's new councillors, and James Cunniff, Stephen's father was made chairperson of the advisory board. A new day had dawned for New Van.

Eventide: Love Is All Around

As September waned, the bustling town of Eventide began to slow down. Those who were staying for the winter were filling their woodsheds and stacking their larders with dried fruits and meats. The root cellars smelled of fall apples and turnip. The mills were still busy but slowing production.

Dubbed Mayor by the people, Richard was busy organizing the free folk—a challenging task in the best of times. He was happy. It had been a good summer. He and Boris, designated as 'Chief' by Richard, ran a tight ship. The militia under Boris had adopted the motto, 'To Serve and Protect.' To this new direction, the townsfolk responded well. Negotiations to continue one more year under the established resource agreement looked promising.

Jana and Anna had become best friends. Sandra was like an older sister to them both. After Anna's children were in bed one cool September night, the three couples sat in Michael and Anna's living room sharing some fresh apple cider. The fire crackled and the room was cozy.

Douglas stood before his friends and announced, "Sandra and I are expecting. In the spring, we will be parents."

Anna burst out, "You won't need any clothes. I saved them all."

Jana held her cider high, "A toast to new friends and a baby in our midst. We are truly blessed."

Upstairs, two little girls poked their heads out the railing. They said in unison, "We will have a new friend to play with." Richard shooed them off to bed.

All smiles, Richard congratulated Douglas. He said, "Perhaps we should pull the cork on the hard cider." He looked over to Sandra, "Sorry, it's straight juice for you."

Haida Gwaii: Island of the People

A solitary boat approached the cove at Long Point. A cloudy day was the norm in the village facing the western ocean. At landing, Chief Commanda, Ahana and her elders were there to welcome the negotiating teams for the island's future. Behind them stood the grand totems. Stephen Cuniff was accompanied by Kate Scott, his fellow representative for the resource Barons of New Van. Following close behind were Starhawk and Anita Freeland, representing the island communities. Ahana hosted the opening session on the sacred territory of Haida Gwaii.

In the longhouse, the sacred gathering place of her people, Ahana opened the session. She asserted her claim of sovereignty over her island of Haida Gwaii. Beside her sat a familiar face. Shania claimed status as a representative of the peoples of the Wilds.

Starhawk took a different stance, claiming the people of the island should control their designated districts as determined by this negotiation. Anita supported this premise, creating a central committee established to settle island disputes.

The delegation from New Van held a very different view. Stephen and Kate insisted the island was large enough for significant resource removal. They asserted that a loose structure of rules to assure forest and fishery renewal was all that was required.

Ahana invited the island delegation to speak. Starhawk held the book high in the air. "Eons ago, our forebearers brought the human race almost to extinction. We now have the opportunity to learn from the errors of our ancestors and to act accordingly. We have time to do things differently."

Anita continued, "We have proof that we can thrive and sustain our environment. Communities, large and small, across our island are learning to live in harmony with nature and each other."

Stephen asked Ahana for the floor. He presented a plea for reason. "The parties we represent require a plan that gives them enough resources to grow their enterprises. Are what they demand and what you want compatible in our world? I sincerely hope the answer is yes." His associate Kate was not comfortable with such a soft reply.

Ahana looked to Shania for her view. Shania reminded all assembled of a simple fact and a caution, "No man or woman should be given the power to claim a territory for any reason when it is already occupied by others. It has happened in the past and I do not believe 'the people' will let it happen again."

Stephen listened and, in his heart, he knew the conspiracy would prevail.

The first meeting to discuss the island's future ended without any clear results. However, there was one very bright spot. All participants except for one agreed to refer to the island as Haida Gwaii. Stephen was confident he had time to sway the dissenting vote. Their island was sacred and its people worth protecting.

Windmill Valley: Our House

After two months of building, Charles' and Angela's A-frame cottage was almost ready. The fireplace had been the stickler. Neighbours assisted when needed, and Sam joined them to complete the job. The furniture would be sparce until the carpenter in Killaloo was free for the winter. However, the house was sturdy, and John had three windows he had acquired from friends in the city. Overlooking the pond, the living room had a rug and two cozy chairs. In the loft was a new bed with all the necessary linens and a quilt.

Near the house, the woodshed was almost full. All of the other needs would be shared by John and Rita until, over time, Charles' and Angela's house was relatively self-sufficient.

They knew they were home. Angela still had the wanderer's need, and Charles was eager to explore his island and to help new communities find their way. They could have both worlds.

One October day, Charles carried Angela over the threshold. John had a bottle of wine to toast the good times. Rita brought a fresh loaf of bread to bring health and prosperity to the new home.

The next morning, Charles woke feeling wonderful. The sun was rising in the eastern sky. The clouds were puffed and but a few. Blue sky in the morning. The sign of a beautiful day. He stood before the window. The robin got the worm and Charles cried, "Hello world. Here I come."

From the bed came a sultry female voice, "Good morning, my love." He reconsidered his plan and went back to bed.

Earthborn: Days of Future Past

Under the tall maple, Tom watched the winds of autumn blow the leaves out over the meadow. He held a new book in his hands. Suzanne had sent him the first draft. It was called 'The Secret Revealed.' Opening it to the first page, Tom read, "Herein lies the story of Earthborn, a meek little village in the centre of the great woods in the middle of a sacred island." He marvelled at the description of his beloved settlement. Wondering why the term meek was used as a descriptor, he read its meaning. One meaning is simply 'patient.' It sat well with Tom. In patience, there is strength and purpose. It allows for frustrations and pitfalls, but it never loses sight of the goal. Tom agreed it suited the nature of Earthborn well.

In the short autumn days, Earthborn returned to its quiet, steady self. Many discussions were held as to the direction Earthborn should take. Most agreed it should remain true to itself. It grew, but slowly, and so it should continue to do so. Visitors would be welcomed, but only to learn and then return to their homes with new ideas and plans for the future.

After all the commotion, it appeared there was a newfound interest in the bigger world. Some, like Raven, were eager to explore a little. Even Tom and Darla planned to visit Abdul's Festival of Love. Visits from the wanderers, Gab and Cody and now Adam, on occasion, were very welcome.

Across the meadow came Robert and Inga, hand in hand. Inga had a special glow about her, and Robert seemed to stand a bit prouder lately. They sat under the big tree with their mentor, and contemplated life. Then Inga giggled and Robert got a silly grin on his face.

"Tom, you are about to become an uncle!" laughed Robert. "In the spring there will be one more soul for us to keep."

The end

An Afterword in Time

On the bench under the old maple, a man, perhaps twenty-nine in years, sat telling tales. Around him were a group of children. Mary, who just turned twelve, would never grow too old to hear a story. Star was still captivated by the tales being told. Now old enough to appreciate the realms of fantasy, Cherry listened intently. Seated together were two young siblings, Ryan and Kim, who had heard good stories from birth, right under this tree. Arriving a short time later, Tracy and Melissa ran across the meadow and sat down beside them. They were family visiting from Windmill Valley.

"The world is a wondrous place," spoke the orator. "I have seen grand canyons a mile wide and a mile deep. Like a pebble beside a vast river, I have sat on the canyon floor, in awe of the beauty around me. I have hiked in mountains where the snow never melts. I have seen sunsets and sunrises over vast oceans. On quiet lakes, I have listened to the silence. I have hugged giant redwoods which touched the sky. Beneath a waterfall, I have stood and hiked the hills and valleys of ancient mountains worn down by the ages. In everglades, I have watched alligators swimming. Over an endless desert, I have sailed in a hot air balloon. Glaciers, I have seen from a tranquil bay. I have lived on your beautiful sanctuary island. On sandy shores, I have looked across a vast lake, felt the sand between my toes and contemplated my existence."

"What story would you like to hear today?" he asked raising his gold-wired glasses.

"Have you ever seen The Rolling Stones?" asked Mary, now an avid reader of ancient musical history.

"Not yet, but in time," said David.

Places and Characters

EARTHBORN

Charles	keeper of the book, nickname Sparkle
Isla	writer and poet
Robert	carefree, adventurous young man
Mary	child
Star	child
Tom	elder
Darla	Tom's wife
Sam	young man
Frodo	his dog
Raven	child
Cherry	child
Carrot	donkey

EVENTIDE

Douglas	mill worker
Sandra	wife and seamstress
Richard	injured forester, organizer
Boris	militia boss

NEW VAN

Stephen	student activist, Black Swan conspirator
James	Stephen's father, lumber baron
John	student, guitar player
Inga	horticultural student
Cedric	actor and conspirator

Richard K	musician
Michael	ex militiaman
Anna	Michael's wife
William	social activist
Rachel Phidd	professor
Rose	pregnant conspirator
Kirk	editor, The Phoenix

NEW LIFE COMMUNITY

Raymond (Abdul)	leader
Barbara (Flower)	Raymond's wife and confidant

NEW HARMONY

Gordon	mayor
Anita Freeland	councillor
Shania	councillor for the Wilds
Amanda	councillor

WANDERERS

Angela (Rosebud)	bringer of the Book
Gab	
Cody	

KILLALOO

Barney	community leader
Cathy	teacher
Josh	miller
Martha	miller's wife
Linda	doctor 'medicine woman'

NEW JERUSALEM	
Abraham	cult leader
Jana	follower/nurse
Adam	follower/wanderer recruit
Naomi	young follower
WINDMILL VALLEY	
John Kanaar	philosopher
Rita	wife
Gertrude	goat
Shanda	border collie
FREE FOLK	
Quiet Sue	free folk teepee dweller
MORNINGSTAR	
Emma	librarian and mother
Suzanne	writer
Starhawk	activist
LONG POINT	
Chief Commanda	Ahana

Song Credits

Hello, I Love You	The Doors
One of These Days	Neil Young
The Times They are a Changing	Bob Dylan
The Day Begins	The Moody Blues
Country Roads	John Denver
Every Picture Tells a Story	Rod Stewart
Let the Sunshine In	The Fifth Dimension
Take It Easy	The Eagles
Brave New World	Steve Miller Band
On the Road Again	Willie Nelson
One Fine Morning	Lighthouse
Keeper of the Key	Perth County Conspiracy
Shelter from The Storm	Bob Dylan
The Early Morning Rain	Gordon Lightfoot
Teach Your Children	Crosby, Stills and Nash
Do You Believe in Magic	The Lovin' Spoonful
Good Times Bad Times	Led Zeppelin
Going Back to Big Sur	Johnny Rivers
Bad Moon Rising	Creedence Clearwater Revival
Good Vibrations	The Beach Boys
My Sweet Lord	George Harrison
Stardust	Willie Nelson
She's Come Undone	The Guess Who
Hallelujah	Leonard Cohen
Long Time Gone	Crosby, Stills and Nash
You Aint Going Nowhere	Bob Dylan
I Won't Back Down	Tom Petty and the Heartbreakers
Brothers in Arms	Dire Straits

Stand By Me	Ben E, King
With A Little Help From My Friends	The Beatles
King of the Road	Hank Williams
Father and Son	Cat Stephens
For What It's Worth	Buffalo Springfield
Turn, Turn, Turn	The Byrds
You Can't Always Get What You Want	The Rolling Stones
Monster	Steppenwolf
Life Is A Carnival	The Band
When I Was Young	The Animals
All I Really Want to Do	Bob Dylan
Your Time Is Gonna Come	Led Zeppelin
We're Not Gonna Take It	The Who
We Shall Overcome	Spiritual
Tiptoe Through the Tulips	Tiny Tim
Brown-eyed Girl	Van Morrison
Give Peace A Chance	John Lennon
Tangled Up In Blue	Bob Dylan
I'm Going To The Country	Bruce Cockburn
Sugar Mountain	Neil Young
Woodstock	Joni Mitchell
Share The Land	Guess Who
Imagine	John Lennon
Here Comes the Sun	George Harrison
The Field of Opportunity	Neil Young
Love Is All Around	The Troggs
Wagon Wheel	Bob Dylan
Reason To Believe	Rod Stewart
Our House	Graham Nash
Days Of Future Past	The Moody Blues

CPSIA information can be obtained
at www.ICGtesting.com
Printed in the USA
LVHW010049141220
674086LV00015B/242/J

9 780228 839996